The Daughters Daring

Steven J. Thompson

STEVEN J. THOMPSON

For information about the book and the author visit:
www.daughtersdaring.com

ISBN 978-0-9967232-0-6

Illustrations by Steve Ferchaud

Cover Design by Cindy Grundsten

Printed in the United States of America

First U.S. Edition

Acknowledgements

Let me start by thanking you, the reader, for stopping to glance at this page before jumping into the main adventure. As a reader I can't tell you how many times I've skipped the acknowledgements to get right to the story. Now that I'm speaking as a writer I have a new perspective.

Books aren't easy to publish. They're downright difficult. It can take months to a year just to write your manuscript. Then you go to editing, illustrating, cover design, distribution options, marketing, etc. The list goes on and on. The writer learns that it's not a fun process if you try to go it alone.

Fortunately there are people out there who can help. People like Lynn Tosello, my editor. There's Steve Ferchaud who did the wonderful illustrations so meticulously. There's Alter Ego Costumes in Chico, CA, that provided the dresses worn by my cover models (my own courageous daughters). Then there's Cindy Grundsten, a digital artist in Sweden who finished the cover design along with Cedar Creek Publishing in Paradise, CA who designed the title print. Thanks also to

Marci Shadd of Click & Bloom photography for making me look good in pictures.

I owe a lot of thanks to the North State Writers, a chapter of the California Writers Club. It was through monthly meetings at this club that I met many of the people who helped me finish this book. It was also at these meetings that I found the inspiration to keep going when I was ready to trash bin the whole project. Special thanks to writers T. E. Watson and Ken Young for all of their encouragement.

Thanks also to all of my fans who supported my Gofundme campaign to raise funds for getting this book off the ground. I'm blessed to have so many generous friends and family. Thanks to all my battle buddies in my army reserve unit for believing in me. Drill Sergeants lead the way.

Most importantly I need to thank my family. There are my daughters, the inspiration of my title characters, Emily & Elizabeth Daring. These were characters we made up when my girls were little and still demanded bed time stories from their dad. They are both brave and adventurous and full of eagerness for life. I hope they, and their little brother, never lose that.

Finally my wife Angela, for helping me with book design and pushing me to write when I just wanted to camp on the couch. Angela is an Army wife who has had to put up with dirty combat boots and a Drill Sergeant in the house for eighteen years now. She knows the burden that is so unique to military spouses and I owe her so much for never giving up on me.

Thank you, all of you. You are the source of my courage, my bravery and my daring.

STEVEN J. THOMPSON

Prologue

Elizabeth Daring stood facing her target. Her arrow was nocked and bowstring drawn back with the fletching touching her upper cheek, just as her father had shown her. Her back was straight and her feet a shoulders-width apart, one in front of the other. Her target stood motionless, a simple disc made of burlap and hay, soaking in the first rays of sun. It was morning in the Kingdom of Highcynder and The Shining City would soon awaken, along with Elizabeth's mother, who wouldn't be pleased to find her daughter gone. She had time for one more shot, so she took aim and counted to three.

One.

Emily Daring hung from the rafters of the large overhang behind her sister. It was meant to provide shade and storage for the King's Archers while training, but it was also a great place for the twelve-year-old to exercise while her younger sister practiced her archery. Unfortunately, while great fun, archery and rafter climbing were looked down upon for young girls of noble upbringing. So they had agreed to sneak in this scandalous fun in the early hours of the morning while most people were still asleep. Highcynder was a beautiful kingdom with lovely people; it just got a bit tiring sometimes. Grownups could be so stuffy, expecting everything to be just-so.

Two.

Elizabeth took a breath.

Nathan Wormington thought Highcynder wasn't at all exciting, that is, until he saw the

Daughters Daring sneaking past the soldiers' barracks and into the training arena. He had been tasked with fetching milk for his mother, fresh from the dairyman, when he had spied the girls (strangely dressed like peasants) and decided that whatever they were doing seemed much more interesting than his current task. And, he was ten years old now, they would certainly want his help if they were doing something important. A chubby boy, he had struggled to keep up, but now he was here, watching Emily Daring swing from the rafters while her sister Elizabeth seemed nowhere in sight. That was when Nathan saw the most beautiful blue and red butterfly.

Three.

Elizabeth hoped to win the confidence of their father, the hero of Highcynder, Duke Daring. Not born a noble, the duke had achieved his title through heroic deeds and legendary adventures (that and marrying their mother, who was cousin to the king). Her father loved archery almost as much as swordsmanship. Elizabeth cared little for swords but loved to shoot. Someday she would convince him to let her shoot in a tournament. She exhaled and focused on her target. As she did, a beautiful red and blue

9

butterfly fluttered past the target. She let it pass, then released the bowstring, letting the arrow fly.

That was when she saw Nathan Wormington.

Elizabeth gasped! She saw the arrow, as if in slow motion hurtling toward the annoying, chubby boy who always seemed to get her in trouble. Oh No! She thought, wishing she had waited a second longer. Nathan ran past the target just as the arrow sailed in, hitting him right in the buttock!

The boy let out a howl that could wake the whole kingdom.

"Elizabeth, what did you do!?" cried Emily from the rafters. She dropped and ran to her sister.

"It wasn't my fault!" Elizabeth answered, "He ran right in front of me!"

Emily glanced at her sister's quiver, relieved to see only training arrows and not the more dangerous broad heads. She quickly ran over to Nathan, who was now thrashing about on the ground trying in vain to reach the source of his pain. If Nathan Wormington was known for anything besides being chubby, it was his very loud voice. He now used it to scream at the top of his lungs! Emily wrestled the boy onto his side and pulled the arrow from his backside while trying to quiet him, but it was too late. She looked up to see several soldiers pouring from the barracks to see what the matter was.

"What in the king's name is going on out here?" The captain of the Guard exclaimed as he approached, "Ah, the Daughters Daring. I should have known."

"Oh boy," Emily said. "Mother is not going to be happy with this one."

STEVEN J. THOMPSON

Chapter 1

The Kingdom of Highcynder sat at the edge of the Crystal Sea, soaking in rays of sunlight like a blooming flower of gold. The king's castle stood at the center of this land, surrounded by beautiful buildings of carved stone and artisan brick. Wealthy merchants and traders flourished here, selling all manner of goods within the great walls that enclosed Alcyndra, or what was commonly known as The Shining City. It came to be known throughout the world of Marcynder as a place of peace and prosperity, and merchants sailed from across the Crystal Sea to sell their exotic wares. For those in Highcynder it was a prosperous time, if not for everyone else.

The people of Highcynder considered themselves to be amongst Marcynder's most enlightened. Despite the appearance of royal tradition, their people enjoyed a relative freedom and equality that was unheard of in other kingdoms. Here men and women alike could hold titles of nobility. Such freedom of trade had been established that even the poorest could earn relative fortunes through ingenuity and hard work. People here were judged on their merit, not the color of their skin, or the social class of their birth.

Still, Highcynder enjoyed upholding some traditions, such as a royal family. King Lamont was known as a fair and just ruler. Having lost his queen to illness before having an heir, it was wondered who would take up the throne when Lamont was gone, or if the throne would be retired. The Council of Knights had discussed a more representative form of government, an idea that was gaining popularity with the people.

While such freedoms made Highcynder prosperous, they also caused distrust among other kingdoms. Tyranny and even slavery existed in lands not so far away. Foreign rulers viewed Highcynder's ways as an insult, or even worse, a threat to their own dynasties. To them, freedom was a dangerous idea that could only spark revolution from those less fortunate. This was especially true for the desert kingdom of Dublari. Built on the edge of the Great Sands and the Sea of Fire, the Dublarian culture was built on slavery and other customs that seemed barbaric to most Cynderians.

Although born of Highcynder, the nation of Newcynder had much to be suspicious of as well. Highcynder had been their motherland, and Alcyndra their capitol, until King Lamont had declared them their own country and cut ties. This had come after great political strife, and the loss of Lamont's wife, but Newcynderians had never forgiven what was seen as a great betrayal. Some still aspired to return and lay claim to the throne.

Still, the people of Highcynder considered themselves relatively safe. To the north were the Craggy Mountains. To the south, beyond the sweetberry fields, lay the Putrid Swale (which the Daughters Daring considered just a fancy name for a stinky swamp). Both were nearly impassable, affording Highcynder a strategic barrier to invading armies. The only two ways to approach Highcynder were by the Crystal Sea, which was guarded by the formidable Royal Navy; or through the Enchanted Forest—an approach of last resort.

The Enchanted Forest was a mystical place, both wondrous and scary for the common folk of Highcynder. Those who dared wander in often ended up either lost, or the victims of strange pranks the forest liked to play, which made it very unpredictable. Items could be pilfered from backpacks; vines could grab you by the feet and hang you upside down; and strange voices could call you from different directions. There were trees so old and tall that one could not see their tops. And there were tales of gnomes, goblins, faeries, and the occasional ogre living within it. Eventually, the king of Highcynder declared the forest off limits to anyone not on official business. Though time passed, the people of Highcynder continued to tell the hair-raising tales of the forest's enchantments so that every generation and every traveler could beware.

There were, however, two young adventurers who did not fear the Enchanted Forest. In fact, it was in the Enchanted Forest that one of the Daring Daughters' most amazing adventures took place. It could even be said that the daughters came to be because of the forest, because their parents had met and fallen in love there. To the sisters, it was a place of beauty and adventure, a vision born of their father's grand stories and a daily sight from their bedchamber window. The Daring manor sat at the very edge of The Shining City that overlooked the forest. Being so close, it seemed to be calling to them—a call they had not yet answered.

⌘

"Ouch!" Cried Emily.

"Hold still," her mother responded, running a brush through Emily's dark curls.

Emily swore this had to be punishment. There was nothing she hated more than having her hair brushed. As beautiful as it was, she would rather have it cut off and be done with such nuisance. Her mother wouldn't hear of it. To heap insult on injury, she sat looking out her window at the Enchanted Forest while enduring her mother's grooming.

Her sister, Elizabeth, giggled and made faces at her when she thought she wasn't noticed.

"Mother," she said, "I really don't see why this is necessary. We're only—ouch—going to the market for a short while, and it's too early to—ouch—see anyone we know anyway."

Her mother was firm. "A young lady does not go out in public with uncombed hair." The Duchess Daring was a lovely woman, with the poise and dignity of her station. As cousin to the king, she bore certain responsibilities that came with the privileges of nobility. She wished to encourage her daughters' creative and outgoing spirits, but first, they had to learn how to properly behave.

Emily was the Daring's first child. When she was born, her father had run through the streets of Highcynder, stopping at every inn and tavern to share the news. If not for his wife, he would have had the baby along to show his pride. The duchess, however, had protectively kept Emily with her (as much for her sanity as her daughter's safety).

Emily had an explorer's heart from her first days in the crib and was always getting into some kind of trouble. Now twelve, almost in her teens, Emily already stood as tall as her mother. She was also as athletic as any of the boys her age, with a love for horseback riding, sparring, and tree-climbing, much to her mother's chagrin.

"Emily," the duchess said, "the Sweetberry Festival is approaching, and your impatient father is craving sweetberry pie. I need you and your sister to go to Whipperpeel's for me—without causing any trouble."

"Did someone say sweetberry pie?" The duke asked, strolling in from the hallway. He had incredible hearing whenever anyone spoke of treats.

"Sweetberries!" A little voice yelled from down the hall. Even from his room, Emily and Elizabeth's younger brother Joseph had an ear for sweets matching his father's.

"Father!" Elizabeth exclaimed, running to hug his waist.

"And how is my notorious little archer today?" he asked.

Elizabeth blushed. It had only been a couple of weeks since her accident with Nathan Wormington, but it was likely she wouldn't hear the end of it anytime soon. Being a younger sister was always harder, at least in her mind. She had two parents and an older sister to constantly remind her of her mistakes.

Elizabeth was also the petite one. Not athletic like her sister, she was sharp-minded and a skilled negotiator, able to melt even her father's stern heart with her sapphire blue eyes. Like many of her stature, she had to rely on her charm and wits to gain attention. If only her wilder exploits weren't so infamous!

"Father," she said, changing the subject, "Mother is sending us to Whipperpeel's Sweets Shoppe for some sweetberry pie!"

"Really?" he asked, his eyes lighting up. "That is a splendid idea!" Just then, he noticed his younger daughter's pose. "But what is this?"

Elizabeth now stared up at him expectantly, arm outstretched, palm up.

"Oh," he said, dropping a coin into her hand.

"Mother asked us to get two," Elizabeth said, keeping her palm out, "on account of your nearly eating the last one all by yourself."

"She did? Oh, well ahem, of course, my dear," he said, dropping more coins.

"Thank you Father," she said. With a quick curtsy, the coins vanished into her pocket as she bolted for the door.

"And where do you think you're going?" her mother asked sternly, brush in hand. "Come here, it's your turn now."

Elizabeth sighed as her older sister stuck out her tongue at her.

Chapter 2

It was a warm and sunny morning and yet the streets of Highcynder seemed strangely quiet. The daughters had passed only a few people on their way to the market district where normally there would have been dozens. Emily, now tugging at her uncomfortable dress, seemed not to mind having less of an audience. The last thing she wanted was to have to stop and talk to all the nobles and recount some adventure of her father's for them, all with a graceful bow at the end.

Elizabeth was relieved as well (especially at not having seen Nathan Wormington's mother), however she was worried. It was too close to the Sweetberry Festival for the capital to be this quiet. Normally there would be signs with streamers proclaiming everybody's favorite time of year. There would be picnic tables in front of shops, and carts and market stalls popping up in every last available space. She couldn't shake the feeling that something was wrong.

Despite the gloomy atmosphere, the daughters were relieved to find that one thing hadn't changed. The smell of baked goods lingering in the air as they rounded the corner to Whipperpeel's Sweets Shoppe. Annie Whipperpeel's bakery was always filled with delicious treats. Just walking in brought the incredible smells of apples and cinnamon, berries, peaches and, sometimes, even rare chocolate! Annie was a delightful lady who always threw in a little something extra when the girls shopped there, too.

Unfortunately, on this day, Annie was out of sweetberries.

"I'm so sorry girls," Annie said, "but I haven't had any sweetberries in a week! No one has. This spring, the bushes were heavy with berries, but now there aren't any. We may have to cancel the Sweetberry Festival."

No sweetberries. That was bad news indeed. The ingredient to father's favorite pie was also one of Highcynder's most treasured treats. People traveled to Highcynder each year for the delectable, burst-in-your-mouth sweetness of the large, purple berries. And the pies were the highlight of the Sweetberry Festival that everyone so loved.

"But what happened to the sweetberries?" Elizabeth asked.

"I don't know. It's the strangest thing," Annie answered, then leaned in to whisper, "But if you ask me, it was those Forest Gnomes what took'em!"

Forest Gnomes! Although Emily and Elizabeth had never seen one, they had heard plenty of stories about them, mostly told by their father at bedtime. Forest Gnomes were not particularly scary, but they were absent-minded and sometimes caused mischief for humans in carrying out their tinkering or grand schemes. Farmers who found their crops planted upside down, or their fences re-crafted into elaborate mazes, even village folk with missing socks, all knew that it had to be those mischievous gnomes! So it wasn't surprising that the gnomes could have taken the sweetberries, but perhaps it was a little odd.

"Why would the gnomes take all the sweetberries?" Emily asked.

"Well," Annie answered, scratching her chin for a moment, "I don't know. They've never done this before, but that doesn't mean anything! Those gnomes are always up to something! Now all the sweetberries in the valley are gone, and I have half a mind to alert the King's Guard about this! Now please excuse me, young ladies, I need to find my spectacles."

Emily and Elizabeth knew that this wasn't a good situation. The missing sweetberry problem was bad enough, but the thought of the King's Guard being alerted was even worse. The King's Guard was the local authority that handled issues too great for the local constable. Their father believed, however, that they used their authority too heavily, often causing more problems than they solved.

"Liz," Emily said, "if the King's Guard gets involved, it won't be very pleasant for the gnomes."

"No," Elizabeth replied, still disappointed that there would be no pie. "But they should have thought of that before they stole all the sweetberries!"

"But how do we know they did it?" Emily retorted. "What if they're innocent? Who is going to stick up for them and help get to the bottom of this?"

Elizabeth's eyes gleamed as she caught on. "You're right! The gnomes are going to need help. They need expert adventurers who know how to present a case to the king and his Royal Guard!"

"Of course they do, Sis. They need the Daughters Daring right away!"

"Now girls," Annie said, reminding them of her presence, "I hope you're not planning to do something that is better left to the authorities."

"Well, um, you see," Emily stammered. Excuses were not her better talent.

"Mrs. Whipperpeel," Elizabeth chimed in, "you know we would never intentionally get into any trouble. We're just going to look around and see if we can solve this mystery for you. You do want the sweetberries found, don't you?"

"Well," Annie answered, "of course I do, dearie. You girls go ahead and ask around the market, but please stay out of that Enchanted Forest!"

"Of course, Mrs. Whipperpeel," Elizabeth answered. "Every child knows the Enchanted Forest is only for the daring or the foolish, and we wouldn't want to be foolish, would we Sis?"

"No, of course not!" Emily answered, catching on to her sister's fun.

"Very well then," Annie said. "Thank you, girls, for finding out what you can. I'm sure I'll be back in the sweetberries and baking pies soon!"

With that, the girls bid her farewell, all the while trying hard not to giggle.

"Elizabeth that was downright cruel of you!"

"Why Emily," Elizabeth answered in a mocking tone, "whatever do you mean?"

"You know what I mean!" Emily responded, as they walked toward home. "You told Mrs. Whipperpeel that the Enchanted Forest was only for the daring or the foolish!"

"Yes, so?"

"So? We are the Darings!"

"And that, Sis, is why we are perfectly qualified to venture into the Enchanted Forest."

"All right, but why?" Emily asked again. "What's in the Enchanted Forest?"

"For starters," Elizabeth answered, "the Forest Gnomes. If we're going to find them, that is where we'll have to start searching."

"Well, in that case," Emily said, picking up her pace, "we're going to need our adventuring gear."

⌘

Highcynder, while grand, wasn't a very large kingdom, and Emily and Elizabeth had explored nearly every inch of it that wasn't locked behind closed doors. They knew the wharf and boat docks, had been to the edge of the Putrid Swale (mother caught them with mud on their knickers that day), and had even hiked with their father around the base of the Craggy Mountains. However, the Enchanted Forest was a place they had not yet explored. Many adults feared to go there and, of course, there was the king's rule that only those on royal business could enter. The daughters decided that their business was certainly of royal importance and therefore the king shouldn't mind this one little peek. In fact, he would probably be thanking them when this was all over, once they found the lost sweetberries!

They rushed home and changed into their "adventuring clothes." Their mother would insist they looked like ragamuffins but Emily was glad just to be out of her stuffy dress. Elizabeth looked at her clothing in a more practical way and, while she enjoyed pretty dresses, they weren't cut out for the adventure at hand.

Not knowing for sure what dangers might be ahead, Emily grabbed her sling-staff as well as a hunting dagger her father had given her. The staff was made of stout oak, with a special cord at the end and a strap of leather attached in the middle. In a pinch, the staff and cord made a strong slingshot that could hurl rocks the size of chicken eggs with ease (It could also hurl actual chicken eggs, which made quite a mess when she tested it, once). The dagger was a work of art with a leather handle and the Daring crest etched on the blade.

Not to be outdone, Elizabeth chose her best bow, along with a quiver of arrows carved just for her smaller size. The bow was of the finest wood and, like Emily's knife, it bore the Daring crest.

The girls filled their packs with bread and dried meat, water, fire flints, and a journal to document their discoveries. They had "adventured" before, although much closer to home, and had watched their father pack many times. While they lacked his sword and armor, they knew what to bring, and were not without their own weapons and wits.

They were almost to the manor gate when their mother stopped them. She was tending her garden, while Joseph played in the grass nearby. It wasn't common for nobles to work in the soil, but the duchess was very particular about her garden and insisted on doing it herself, as she had a sharp eye for details.

"Girls," she queried, "where are you off to dressed like bandits? And where are the pies I sent you for?"

The sisters paused. Emily shrugged her shoulders but Elizabeth quickly answered,

"Duke Archibald's nephews were hoping that Father would come by the royal courtyard and tell another of his adventure stories. We decided that, rather than distract Father from his important duties, we would go and entertain them ourselves with a fabulous make-believe adventure."

Their mother studied them for a moment, not entirely convinced, but not sure if she should press them on it. She worried, as all mothers do, about her two precious girls. They did not always get along, and it was good to see them playing together. She hoped that, someday, they would grow to see the true value of the other, and each appreciate her sister for her beauty and character.

"And the pies?" the duchess asked.

"They were all out," Emily answered, "Annie Whipperpeel said there is a shortage of sweetberries!"

"How odd," the duchess said. "That doesn't bode well for the festival.

"You two go ahead and play, but I warn you. If you get into trouble, I'll put you both in the care of a governess and lock you in your room for a week!"

"Thank you, Mother!" The girls responded in unison, running out the gate and down the path to the royal courtyard. The duchess watched them until they rounded a corner and were out of sight.

What neither the duchess, nor the daughters as they sped away, noticed, was the set of small eyes watching them from the shadows of a nearby hedge.

☐

STEVEN J. THOMPSON

Chapter 3

The path to the Enchanted Forest took the daughters past the royal courtyard and beyond the soldier's barracks where Elizabeth had only too recently caused quite a ruckus. Further up the path sat a guardhouse next to a large gate where two soldiers stood guard. The gate was fortified with large, wooden doors that could be swung shut and barred with a stout, wooden beam. Suspended above the doors, was a rather rusty-looking portcullis, which was simply an iron gate that could be lowered into place giving reinforcement to the wooden doors. In Emily's life she had never seen the doors shut or portcullis lowered. She thought the idea of two guards at a gate that almost no one used seemed silly, but her father had reminded her that, even though this was a postern, or secondary gate, it was important to the safety of the city that it be guarded day and night.

These soldiers posed a problem for the girls. They surely would not permit the daughters of Duke Daring to leave The Shining City without an escort.

"We'll just tell them we are on official business of the king," Elizabeth said.

"Just like that?" Emily said incredulously. "I don't think it will work."

"Trust me."

As the daughters approached the guards, one of them stepped forward. His buckskin uniform was nicely polished and glistened in the sun. He had a big, thick mustache, much like their father's, and Emily thought he looked rather handsome.

"Hello there," he said, "Where might you young ladies be off to today?"

"Hello, good sir," Elizabeth said cheerily. "We are the Daughters Daring and we are on an important mission to help the king."

"To help the king you say?" The guard responded with a slight chuckle. "And what kind of mission are you on?"

"Why, an important mission of much secrecy!" Elizabeth exclaimed.

The guard with the mustache chuckled again, and now his fellow guard was also smiling. The second guard looked younger and had fewer decorations on his tunic, so Emily figured he was probably of lower rank than the mustached man.

"Wait a minute," the second guard said, eyeing them more closely, "aren't you the ones who shot that young boy in the backside with an arrow?"

Emily was starting to worry that her sister's plan wasn't going to work.

"We are the Daughters Daring," Elizabeth repeated, trying to maintain an air of confidence. "That was an unfortunate incident, but the boy is fully recovering. Now, we really must be about our mission, if you don't mind?"

"My dear lady," the mustached man said, "with all due respect to your family, I must say this does seem a bit, irregular. Perhaps we should wait here while I send my corporal to fetch your father and make sure this mission meets his approval?"

Now Emily was really worried.

"Now look," Elizabeth started to answer, when a small rock bounced off the second guard's helmet.

"What the blazes was that?" he exclaimed.

The mustached guard raised his index finger to the daughters and turned his attention to the foliage outside the gate. He stepped forward, looking this way and that, trying to detect their assailant. He ducked as another rock whizzed past him, again hitting the second guard, this time on the bridge of his nose.

"Yeeooowww!!!" he cried out.

"To arms, coward!" The mustached guard yelled, drawing his sword and charging into a nearby thicket. The second guard, now in great pain, had his hands over his face and was stomping his feet. Both guards had forgotten about the daughters.

"Come on, Sis!" Elizabeth whispered.

The daughters sped past the second guard, out the gate, and off in the opposite direction of the mustached guard. Most of the area around them was an open field, but there were a few stands of trees that they could use to stay hidden. After they ran beyond the nearest thicket, no one seemed to be following them, and they slowed down.

"What happened back there?" Emily asked her sister.

"I don't know," Elizabeth said, looking back. "Someone was helping us, not that I needed any help, but who?"

"And why?" Emily said.

The daughters decided it was a mystery best solved later, after they found the missing sweetberries. They rounded another stand of trees and came to an old trail. Although grown over, it was clear from the trampled foliage that it had been used recently, and by numerous sets of feet. They didn't have to follow the trail very far before they came upon the Enchanted Forest.

"This is it, Liz. Once we go in, there's no turning back."

"Really, Em, you're soooo dramatic! What's the worst that can happen?"

With characteristic daring, the girls entered the forest. Emily hefted her staff for extra comfort, while Elizabeth gripped the handle of her bow. As they walked, their confidence grew as they beheld the many sights of the beautiful forest. There were majestic trees that seemed to reach up into the heavens, vines and flowers of every sort, colorful butterflies that danced softly in the air. This certainly did not seem like a place of danger.

After a while, Elizabeth spotted a crushed sweetberry on the trail, and Emily found tiny footprints just beyond that. The girls agreed it had to be the footprints of gnomes, and they followed them farther into the forest, until the trail lead them to the entrance of a large, dark cave. The forest was quiet here, and the air coming from the cave was chilly. They tried peering in, but couldn't see very far for the limited light. Emily started gathering small sticks and bundled them together to make a torch.

"Well," Emily said, "the trail clearly leads here. I guess we should check it out."

"All right," said Elizabeth, "but you hold the torch. I need two hands for my bow."

Emily gave her sister a look. "Fine, just be careful. I would hate to get shot in the backside!"

"Oh please! Do I have to hear about it endlessly? He ran right in front of me, and his chubby backside was impossible to miss!"

Emily shook her head at her sister and started into the cave. Elizabeth followed closely behind, an arrow nocked on her bow.

The cave was damp and not very inviting. The girls agreed this didn't seem like a pleasant place for gnomes to live. Still, neither of them had ever visited the homes of gnomes before, so they couldn't be sure.

They ventured on for a while and soon Elizabeth lost interest. While Emily was carefully tiptoeing, her sister (having returned the arrow to her quiver) made sport of jumping from rock to rock. This was fun, and she was enjoying herself quite well, until she stepped on a wobbly rock that was covered in moss, and slipped. The rock spun out from under her, dumping her on her own backside with a thud. The rock rolled into the darkness, falling down a crevice and bouncing loudly off several other large rocks in its path.

Something in the distance grumbled.

The girls froze, trembling as they tried to listen into the darkness. Whatever had grumbled sounded big, much bigger than a gnome. After a few moments, Emily sighed, ready to press on.

Then, there was a different noise. This was a lighter sound, like raindrops, or maybe the sound of hundreds of tiny feet. It grew louder.

"Somethings coming!" Emily shouted. "Run!"

The girls raced back out of the cave and into the forest where they could see their surroundings better. Emily dropped the torch and already had a good, round stone loaded up on the end of her staff. Elizabeth aimed her bow into the mouth of the cave, her arrow ready.

"Liz," said Emily, her voice tight. "We don't want to kill them!"

"I know that," answered Elizabeth, somewhat breathless. "I'm using the safety arrows Father gave me. Wooden tip, see? It won't harm them, but it will hurt!"

Seconds later, the first of the small creatures emerged from the cave, but instead of gnomes they were goblins! They were small, like gnomes, standing about as tall as Elizabeth. Their skin had a green hue, and their eyes were beady black. Some of them carried crude weapons made of sharp rocks bound to wooden handles. Others carried daggers or sharpened sticks. All of them seemed menacing.

Goblins naturally tried to avoid sunlight, so they wore hooded cloaks to give cover from the sun. The light of the forest disoriented them as they first exited the cave, but one soon spotted the girls and screamed at them.

Whoooosh! Elizabeth's arrow hit the goblin square in the forehead, its blunt tip knocking the creature senseless.

Whack! A rock from Emily's staff sent another goblin to its knees.

The girls continued hurling missiles at the small, green creatures, but now the goblins knew where their enemy was, and moved to surround them. Emily grabbed Elizabeth and was ready to retreat, when the sound of a new commotion arose behind them.

"Gnomes!" Emily shouted as she looked back.

A large group of actual gnomes had arrived and were moving to outflank the goblins. Several gnomes quickly set up a strange contraption while others guarded them. It was a square platform with a seat in the middle, a hand crank attached to gears and pulleys, several poles with what looked like cups on the end, and on the platform, a basket of rocks.

When the contraption was finished, one of the gnomes took his place in the seat and started the hand crank, while others loaded rocks into the pole cups. He yelled, "Firing!" Almost immediately, rocks the size of goose eggs started rapidly hurling at the goblins, smashing into them and knocking them off their feet. Faced with this weapon, the goblins started retreating into the cave.

A group of gnomes, on the other side of the girls, collided with other goblins, pushing them back with small staves and strange, handheld weapons that seemed to shock the creatures with magical energy. Puzzled, and fearful of the strange weaponry, these goblins retreated, as well. With hisses and squeals, they scurried into the depths of the cave.

Once the last of the goblins had disappeared into the cave, the gnomes turned to face the girls. A gnome with frizzled gray hair and a wrinkled face approached the daughters. "Who are you, and what are you doing in our forest?"

STEVEN J. THOMPSON

Chapter 4

"No, the question is: Who are you?" Emily countered, ready to launch another rock at the army of gnomes surrounding them.

The old gnome grunted and said, "We're the Forest Gnomes. My name is Randolph, I am the leader of the Forest Gnomes. Well, we don't actually have titles of authority, but I am the "unofficial" leader as it were. It all started one day when the Gnomish High Council got together and realized that we had no official leadership. Even the high council was just a gathering of any gnome who chose to show up to meetings, which was usually any gnome who wasn't already engaged elsewhere. Say, those eyes are familiar, by any chance are you related to Duke Daring?"

Elizabeth stepped forward, amazed that the gnome had stopped to take a breath. "Yes, he is our father. We are the Daughters Daring. But you already knew that, didn't you?"

Randolph looked surprised and all the gnomes behind him began to whisper quietly to each other. It had been a while since gnomes had actually talked to humans, let alone two who were related to Highcynder's most famous hero!

"Yes, Daughters Daring," Randolph answered. "Your suspicions are correct. We have been watching you today."

"And you helped us at the gate?" Elizabeth asked.

"Yes, that was our doing." Randolph said.

"Why?"

Randolph hesitated a moment and scratched his little white beard. Emily thought he looked quite distinguished for such a peculiar little fellow.

"We need your help, Daughters Daring," He answered. "We thought at first your people had taken all the sweetberries and left none for ourselves. We see now that we were wrong."

"When we saw your plight," Randolph continued, "we realized it was something worse."

"You mean the goblins?" Emily asked.

"Yes, and no," he said. "We discovered the goblins took the sweetberries, but they are not acting alone. They have a plan, which they couldn't have come up with by themselves."

"Who then?" Elizabeth asked.

"The Ogre King," Randolph said.

Several gnomes gasped at the name. Emily and Elizabeth had heard of him, as well, through their father's stories. The fiercest and meanest of all the ogres, he was said to be as tall as two men, and ate horses for snacks. He had been banished to the Craggy Mountains, almost a decade before, by Duke Daring and a band of adventurous knights.

"Why would the Ogre King take our sweetberries?" Emily asked. "He must know we will find him out and our king will send more knights to defeat him."

"This time, he is aided by a witch," Randolph said. "Our scouts have not seen her, but we have recognized her dark presence. Sweetberries add a certain potency to any magical concoction they are mixed with, especially sleeping potions. That would make them valuable to her."

"How would sweetberries play any part in a sleeping potion?" Elizabeth asked.

Emily stood quietly thinking it over. She had set her backpack down to relax her shoulders. "Well, Liz, are you sure it's impossible? It does seem like every time I eat Sweetberry Pie I am sleepy afterward. Maybe the witch is magnifying their ability to make you relaxed and sleepy."

Elizabeth looked surprised, as if this was the last thing she expected Emily to say.

"Don't look at me that way, Elizabeth! I can be just as smart as you are."

"I didn't say anything!" Elizabeth said defensively. "Any way, of course you know everything that has to do with food." She snickered at her own retort, while Emily stuck out her tongue in response.

Meanwhile, Randolph was standing with crossed arms and was impatiently tapping his foot. Several other gnomes had started exploring their surroundings, picking up rocks and examining flowers. Two of them were in an argument about how many goblins it would take to light a candle. This joke seemed very strange to Elizabeth, as she had not heard it before. It was apparent to her that gnomes were very easily distracted.

"This is wasting time!" Randolph growled.

"All right," Emily responded, "if the Ogre King has the sweetberries, where do we find him so we can get them back?"

"It won't be so easy," Randolph said. "You may have your father's courage, but the Ogre King is a fierce creature! Knights have fallen before him."

"Hmmm," Emily considered. "Perhaps we should go to Father and—."

"Fierce creature my boot!" Elizabeth interrupted boldly. "He has yet to cross paths with the Daughters Daring! Besides, we're not going to confront him openly, anyway."

"We're not?" Emily asked, not quite getting the whole idea, but she could tell her sister was up to something.

"Of course not," answered Elizabeth, glad to have everyone's attention. "Ogres may be fierce, but they're not the sharpest swords in the scabbard, as Father would say. They're actually not very bright at all. We are going to sneak in and take the sweetberries right out from under his ugly old nose!"

"Sneak in?" Emily was beginning to think her sister might have fallen on her head, back in the cave. "We'll more likely be captured and eaten with that plan! That is the stupidest idea I have ever heard of!!"

Emily's words stung Elizabeth. Sometimes sisters could be your best friend, and other times say some of the meanest things. Elizabeth prided herself on her wits and felt her anger growing. She was especially hurt that her sister would say such a thing in front of the gnomes.

"Is not!" Elizabeth shot back. "You're just jealous that you didn't think of it first! You're jealous that I am smarter than you!"

"I am not jealous!" Emily yelled. "You are jealous that I am older and have more privileges. And I'm better at sports!"

"You're better at sports because you act like a boy. It's no wonder Father calls me his little princess! You have the poise of a farm boy!"

"Take that back!" Emily cried. Her sister's words had found their mark. Her eyes were starting to sting with tears.

"I will not!" Elizabeth answered, defiantly. "Why don't you just go back home; I can clearly do this without you getting in the way!"

"Fine!" Emily screamed. "I hope the goblins get you and take you away! My life was much better before you showed up!"

Both sisters now felt the sting of harsh words. Elizabeth threw up her shoulders with a "hmmph," and turned down the trail past the goblin cave. Emily turned the other way, practically knocking over several gnomes as she picked up her pack and stormed off into the forest.

"This is not good," Randolph fretted. "Not good at all."

STEVEN J. THOMPSON

Chapter 5

Emily was walking farther into the forest, down another path she had found, angrily kicking stones and not paying much attention to where she was going. She was thinking of the mean things Elizabeth had said to her. Little sisters could be so disagreeable! Emily was just as capable and smart as she needed to be, and smart enough to know when one of Elizabeth's schemes was too dangerous for them.

The thought of danger had just started her thinking about the forest, again, when she heard a soft crunching sound behind her. She turned around but saw nothing, and the noise stopped.

She had only taken a few steps when 'the noise returned. "Who's there?" She demanded, whirling around but still finding no one there. She gripped her staff more tightly.

"Hullo," said a small voice. Again, it sounded like it came from behind her. Emily spun around, determined to confront whoever was following her. The path was bare.

"Where are you?" Emily asked, still annoyed with her sister and growing impatient with this voice.

"In here," the voice said. Now it sounded somewhat muffled, but very close to her ear.

Realizing where it came from, Emily removed her backpack and opened it. Inside she found a tiny gnome helping himself to some of her snacks. This gnome had red shoes and a noticeable pot belly, probably from eating other people's snacks.

"Hey! How'd you get in there?" Emily demanded.

"Oh, terribly sorry," the gnome answered, "but after the ruckus with the goblins, I was fatigued and hungry. This looked like a comfortable place to enjoy a quick nap, and I was so delighted to find that you had food in here, as well!"

"And I see you helped yourself to it," Emily said, a little perturbed. "Who are you, anyway? And, if I may ask, why are you so much smaller than the other gnomes?"

"Apologies again, Miss Daring. My name is Periwinkle!" he said, bowing as well as he could from his cozy spot among her snacks. "And I am a garden gnome! We're not as big as our forest gnome cousins, but we are quite resourceful."

"I see. Well, hello, Periwinkle. Would you mind getting out of my backpack?" Emily was trying her best to be cordial.

"Hmm?" Periwinkle responded, while absently munching on a biscuit. "Oh, actually, I'm quite comfortable in here, and was hoping I could stay a while."

Emily frowned and was ready to dump him out, when she heard a scream in the distance.

"My sister's in trouble!" Emily took off running toward the scream, tossing her backpack, and the small gnome in it, onto her back in one quick motion. "Hang on Liz," she called out as she ran, "I'm coming!"

Emily cut through the forest now, leaving the path and her earlier annoyance behind. She did not know that leaving a path in the Enchanted Forest was never a wise choice. Though plenty of paths lead safely, this way and that, once off the paths, it was easy to become lost, or worse.

She had run in the direction of her sister's screams, but it seemed the sound was moving farther away. She stopped and turned around, but nothing in the forest seemed familiar. Something was not right, she thought. Even the trees seemed to move whenever she looked away.

Emily heard the scream again, and was sure of the direction, this time. A wall of vines hung between her and her sister. She plunged straight in, hoping to push her way through to the other side, but the vines would not budge. Even worse, they started wrapping around her, ensnaring her arms and legs and actually lifting her off the ground until she was bundled like a package and hanging in mid-air.

And then came the goblins.

"Here's another fine mess Elizabeth has gotten me into," she muttered to herself, as they carried her away.

⌘

Elizabeth had been dealing with her own problems since leaving her sister and the bothersome gnomes. First, she had wasted her time on a trail that seemed to lead in endless circles. She had also failed to find any more clues, not even a single dropped sweetberry! Worst of all, she could hear her sister yelling in the distance, calling her name at the top of her lungs. What was wrong with her? Did she want to alert the entire goblin army of their location?

Elizabeth's boldness increased as she walked. She didn't really need her sister along to solve the sweetberry mystery, but her mother would be very cross if she came home alone, even if she single-handedly saved the kingdom, which she was sure would be the outcome. For now, she would just have to rescue her bumbling sister and hope that she did not get in the way.

Elizabeth headed in the direction of her sister's loud yelling, but much as Emily had experienced, she found the voice hard to pinpoint. She wandered this way and that, sure she was getting closer, until the direction of the voice changed again.

She stopped and tried to remember the tales about the Enchanted Forest, which was known for magical mischief on unsuspecting wanderers. She closed her eyes, let out a deep sigh, and tried to use all of her senses. She felt a light breeze on her skin, could hear a bird chirping in the distance, and she smelled— something putrid.

It was the smell of goblins.

Elizabeth had no sooner readied her bow with an arrow than several goblins popped out of the forest, surrounding her. As they threw a small hunting net over her, she screamed for her sister, but it was too late. They bundled her up, and two of them carried her away over their shoulders.

"This is all Emily's fault," she complained to herself, as they carried her down into another entrance to the cave.

Chapter 6

Being smaller creatures, standing no taller than Elizabeth, it took three goblins to carry Emily into the lower reaches of the cave before dropping her, rather abruptly, onto the floor of a large wooden cage. One of them muttered something about how heavy she was and kicked her leg. Emily had discovered that her legs were unbound and returned the favor. She kicked him in the backside, sending him crashing into his cohorts.

The three goblins stumbled, and fell outside of the cave. Two of them started yelling at the one Emily had kicked, but this one was busy shaking a fist at her. She hoped that perhaps, in the confusion, they would forget to lock the door of her cage, but she had no such luck. They quickly locked her in and went about their business. Two more goblins guarded the entrance to this section of the cave, which was a small, oval-shaped room.

Emily assessed her surroundings. There was a torch on the cave wall but it wasn't providing much light. She would need time for her eyes to adjust. She could also just make out a strange figure that was laying down inside the cage. The figure exhaled.

"Who's there?" Emily demanded.

"Em?" a small, familiar voice answered, "It's me!"

"Liz! It is you!" Emily rushed to grab her sister up in a tight hug.

"Ugh," Elizabeth groaned, "you're squishing me!"

Emily stepped back, looked her sister over, and grinned. "Are you ok? Before I was captured I heard you scream."

Elizabeth shrugged off Emily's concern. "I'm fine. I thought I heard you scream, too, but I realized too late it was those nasty goblins."

"They got me, too," said Emily. "I was really worried about you."

Not one to be sentimental, Elizabeth insisted, "I told you I'm fine. We shouldn't be fussing over that anyway. We need to find a way out of here."

Emily agreed but decided that she would check on her sister later, after they were free of their cage. "So, have you already searched for any weak spots—any place that we could escape through?"

Elizabeth shook her head, "No, I've searched top to bottom and I can't find anything."

Emily peered at their enclosure. "Search again. There has to be a weak point. Goblins aren't exactly known for their craftsmanship."

"What you say there?" One of the goblins approached the cage with his hands on his hips. "What you know about goblin cage? Goblins make best cage. No escapes!"

"Eww! What's your name, Stink Eye?" Elizabeth said and Emily began laughing. The goblin Elizabeth had called Stink Eye had one bulging eye, drooping and gooey. While Emily was bent over laughing, she noticed that the other goblin had an unattractive trait of his own.

"Hairy Foot!" she gasped before laughing even harder.

The two goblins stared wide-eyed at the girls. Then they turned to look at each other with suspicion.

"How the human know your name Hairy Foot?" Stink Eye asked in a demanding whisper.

Hairy Foot's eyes grew wide. "How they know your name Stink Eye?" He looked even closer at his companion. "You traitor! I knew it! I knew it! You traitor!" Hairy Foot was bouncing up and down shouting his accusations.

"Me traitor? You traitor!" Stink Eye yelled, lunging to pounce on Hairy Foot. The two goblins went rolling on the cave floor, tossing this way and that.

Emily finally stopped laughing and looked over at her sister, who was watching the fight, cheering on Stink Eye. The sight of the goblins rolling around, hitting and gouging each other, was both funny and frightening. For the moment, the goblins were preoccupied and ignoring the girls in the cell.

"Elizabeth, this is our chance to find a way out," Emily said, pulling Elizabeth away from the cage bars. Both girls went back to scouring their prison cell for a way out. They were busy pulling on the cage bars when they heard the klink of metal on stone.

One of the goblins had dropped a ring of keys as the two of them scuffled around the room. Emily and Elizabeth carefully moved to the bars nearest to the keys. Each tried reaching them, but even Emily's longer arms were not long enough to touch the keys. Their efforts went unnoticed. Stink Eye was chasing Hairy Foot into the darkness of the passageway. Their goblin grunts and yowls grew fainter by the moment.

"They're gone now," Elizabeth said.

"Yeah, but we can't reach the keys! What are we going to do?"

The girls were stumped. The keys were out of reach and so was their gear. Emily's staff was sitting along the wall next to Elizabeth's bow and both of their backpacks.

Emily looked again at her backpack. Even in the dim light, she could see it moving.

"Liz, look at my pack!"

"Eeeew, there's a rat in your backpack!" Elizabeth shivered at the thought.

"It's not a rat, silly!" Emily said.

"What is it, then?"

"You'll see." Emily fished in her pocket and pulled out a round stone. "This is my last one," she said, holding it in her palm for Elizabeth to see."

Elizabeth was amazed at her sister. "How did you get that in here?"

"Let's hope I can hit my pack!"

"I'm sure you can," Elizabeth said, "but what's in the pack that can help us?"

"Be quiet while I aim!"

Emily cocked her arm back and hurled the stone straight at the pack, hitting it with a dull thud.

"Ow!" A little voice cried out from inside the pack. As the girls watched, tiny hands, then a head, popped out of the backpack.

"Not very nice to be throwing things at me," the gnome said.

"Periwinkle!" Emily said, trying to whisper. "Get the keys and help us get out of here!"

"Oh, very well," Periwinkle said. "But if you're not nice to me, I'll crawl back into my new home and take a long nap!"

"Your home?" Emily said, somewhat annoyed. Elizabeth had to restrain her sister from saying anything more, lest the gnome change his mind. He scuffled over to the keys and handed them to Elizabeth.

"Why are you so small?" Elizabeth asked him.

"I am a Garden Gnome, cousin to the Forest Gnomes." Periwinkle answered.

"And they're very resourceful." Emily chimed in.

"I see." Elizabeth responded.

Within moments, the girls were out of the cage, their gear back in hand. Periwinkle had decided to ride in Emily's backpack again, and in no time, they could hear him snoring.

"Seriously, Em," said Elizabeth, "you keep gnomes in your backpack, now?"

"Oh stop," Emily answered, but before she could continue her defense, she noticed a heap of cloth on the floor. "Look here! Those goblins left their cloaks. We can use them as a disguise!"

"You're too tall to be a goblin, Em," Elizabeth said. "And these things smell terrible!"

"Just put one on."

Soon they were both dressed as goblins, and had rubbed some dirt on their faces to be more convincing. With weapons in hand, they headed back into the main corridor of the cave. No sooner had they left the cage room, than they passed two different goblins headed the other way. They passed by without a second glance!

"See?" Emily whispered.

"Oh all right, your plan worked," said Elizabeth, softly. "But you still don't look like a goblin."

Emily swept her sister up in another hug.

"Eeew," said Elizabeth, louder than she'd intended to be, "you smell like one, though!"

The girls cupped their hands over their mouths to quiet a fit of giggles. Now it was time to get serious. They had to find the sweetberries.

THE DAUGHTERS DARING

Chapter 7

As the girls made their way deeper into the earth, the passage widened into an enormous cavern. It was huge, at least twice as large as the king's horse arena, and the ceiling must have been at least fifty feet high. Elizabeth saw bats nestled there in the hanging rock formations, and shuddered. Below the bats were scores of goblins (Emily guessed one hundred), many of them humming strange tunes as they worked.

Along one wall of the cave were baskets and baskets of sweetberries.

There seemed to be three groups of goblins. One group was mashing sweetberries in wooden bowls, while another was mixing in what Elizabeth identified by its scent as valerian root. Finally, the bowls went to the last group who mixed in sugar, then carried the bowls to a doorway leading to what had to be a kitchen.

"Valerian root is used in sleeping potions," Elizabeth said. "I read it in one of Mother's books."

"Then they're making pies with the sweetberries to put people to sleep," said Emily. "But who are they for?"

"And who is baking the pies?" Elizabeth added. "Goblins aren't known for their tasty desserts. Someone else must be in that kitchen."

"Look, there," Emily whispered, pointing.

As one of the goblins delivered a bowl to the kitchen, an even smaller creature, suspended in air, took the bowl and flew back inside. The small, winged creature was glowing weakly, but with a mesmerizing light.

"Of course!" Elizabeth exclaimed in whispered delight. "Fairy Folk!"

"Faeries?" Emily questioned, "Why would they help the goblins?"

"They must not have a choice," said Elizabeth. "Did you see how weak that one looked? I think someone has captured them and is forcing them to do this."

"Probably the witch," Emily said, gripping her staff. "We need to free those poor faeries and make her pay!"

"Not yet, Em," said Elizabeth. "We still need to find out where the Ogre King and that nasty witch are."

A sudden commotion spread across the cave as the Ogre King stepped into the main cavern.

"There he is!" Emily said, her eyes wide.

"Shhhhhh," Elizabeth cautioned. "Someone will hear you!"

Goblins were scattering out of his way. One stumbled in front of him. The huge brute kicked the goblin like a stone and sent him bouncing across the cave, crashing into one of the sugar mixers, causing another commotion as these goblins argued over the mess.

The girls were stunned at the sight of him. The Ogre King was huge; he was taller even than their father and some of the tallest knights in the kingdom. He was also thick like a burled tree trunk, with skin that looked almost like bark. He tossed crates around the room and bellowed about being hungry, while goblins skittered in all directions. Finding nothing but sweetberries, he threatened to start eating faeries.

He stopped, when an icy voice sliced through the din from above. "Oafish fool!"

Emily soon realized the sound came from an opening in the cave ceiling. She could see strange lights, and spidery webs there.

"You will not touch the faeries," the voice continued. "There will be plenty to dine on when the king is under our control and you sit upon his throne."

The Ogre King grumbled and went back to the room where he had been sleeping. The goblins quickly returned to their work, not wishing to draw the attention of the witch, who was clearly watching them from her chamber, above.

"OK Liz," Emily whispered, "what's your plan?"

"One of us needs to get to the kitchen and find a way to free those faeries," Elizabeth said. "I'll go, because I'm smaller and look more like a goblin. Stop giggling."

"OK, and what should I do?" Emily said, barely containing herself.

"When I give the signal, you cause a distraction."

⌘

Elizabeth walked past the first row of goblins, who were busy mashing the sweetberries. She could smell the delicious berries and really wanted to reach out for a handful, but she knew that was a bad idea. The cave was brighter than the tunnel they'd come through, and she feared these goblins would get a better look and realize she didn't fit in. To her surprise, the goblins seemed to ignore her as she walked past them. There were goblins everywhere, busy with myriad tasks. To them, she was just another busy goblin.

After passing seemingly endless rows of goblins, Elizabeth had almost reached the kitchen when a goblin suddenly stepped in front of her. This goblin wore several beaded necklaces around her neck. She wore them with an air of importance, and the others seemed to shy away from her. Elizabeth guessed she must be a chief.

"You!" the goblin chief growled, pointing at her. "Where you going?"

"To kitchen, need supplies." Elizabeth spoke in a low and grumbly voice. The goblin cast a suspicious glance over her, looking her up and down. Elizabeth tensed, believing she'd been caught, and her plan had failed.

Just then, a small round rock smashed into a mixing bowl of sweetberries, mere feet from the two of them. The goblin mixing the berries squealed as crushed berries and juice splashed over its head, right onto the goblin chief. The chief immediately began yelling, beads flying, while chasing the poor mixer goblin around the cave, shaking her fist and threatening all sorts of nasty punishments.

"Thanks, Sis," Elizabeth mouthed the words quietly as she hurried on into the kitchen.

"You're welcome," Emily whispered back. From her vantage point, she could see that her sister had been in trouble. She also was able to make the perfect shot to create the necessary distraction. Now she would just have to wait for Elizabeth's signal.

Watching the scene intently, Emily noticed movement at the edge of the cave. But when she looked closer, she saw nothing. Then, before she looked away, she saw it again. There, in the dark corner of the cave, was a small creature, moving slowly into position near the goblins.

It was a gnome!

As Emily looked around, she started seeing more gnomes. They were coming down from the ceiling on ropes, and coming in from small cracks in the walls. They were wearing dark clothing, and carrying more ropes and weapons over their backs. They were surrounding the goblins and getting into attack formations!

Oh no, Emily thought, if they attack now they'll ruin everything! Liz will be trapped!

Meanwhile, Elizabeth had successfully reached the kitchen and was face-to-face with a fairy—an honest-to-goodness, real, live fairy. She had read about them, but never thought she'd actually see one. This one was enchantingly beautiful, but under the circumstances, very sad. It only gave off a weak light. It was as if these poor creatures were shackled in sorrow and despair. Their lights seemed to be going out! But that would soon change, if Elizabeth could help it.

This fairy was hovering, perhaps a foot from the ground. She had to be only about a foot tall, if that. Her wings, normally described as looking like a butterfly's, now more resembled a dull, brown moth's. The fairy looked up at her and cast an odd glance. "You're a little tall for a goblin, aren't you?" The fairy asked sluggishly.

"No," Elizabeth answered, pulling back her hood so they could see her face, "I'm Elizabeth Daring and I'm here to rescue you!" She quickly surveyed this new cave room. It had been fashioned into a kitchen, with a row of wood-fired ovens and tables covered in Sweetberry Pies. There were a dozen more faeries, all acting as confused and groggy as the first one, making and enchanting pies in a tired, disheartened manner. None of them were smiling or glowing as in the books she had read.

Elizabeth was beginning to feel drowsy, herself, when she noticed a strange orb hanging from the center of the ceiling. It was melon-sized, and its appearance changed from glass to stone, then back to glass. Dark energy and smoke roiled within it like vapors in a teapot, waiting to burst forth. Elizabeth found that the longer she stared at it, the less she cared about the faeries, or her sister, or anything.

Elizabeth decided that this must be the source of the strange spell that hung over the faeries, and could sap her will, too. She reached into her quiver and found the arrow with the strongest broad head. This one was steel, meant for a more dire purpose than her training arrows.

She nocked the arrow and drew the bowstring back, stretching it to its limit. She waited to aim until the last moment, not daring to look too long at the orb, lest it capture her will. Even now, it reached into her mind, compelling her to relax and surrender. It was sapping her will and her arms trembled, but all she had to do was let go of the string.

Elizabeth's arrow flew true. It smashed into the orb with a loud cracking sound and bounced to the stone floor, below. The orb broke open and the dark energy inside flowed, snakelike, around the room before flying out the doorway. Elizabeth felt her strength and resolve return as soon as it left.

"Thank you," the first fairy said. Her color was already returning, along with her glow. "What was your name, again?"

"Elizabeth Daring."

"Daring?" Another fairy asked, flying over to them. "Oh my, yes," she said. "You look so much like your mother!"

"I've been told that," Elizabeth said, "But how do you know my mother?"

An angry, venomous scream pierced the moment's calm.

"The witch!" exclaimed the faeries.

"Come on," Elizabeth said, "We have to get you out of here!"

One of the faeries pointed to the corner "There's a venting tunnel that leads outside!"

A bellowing roar echoed through the cave. It was louder than any goblin.

"Oh no, the ogre has awakened!" The faeries fluttered about in alarm.

Elizabeth turned her attention to the vent. A crude grate covered the opening. The ogre's advancing steps seemed to shake the whole room. Elizabeth kept her mind on the vent and managed to pry the grate off. The faeries quickly flew into the tunnel.

"Come with us," the last fairy said, beckoning to her.

"I can't fit," Elizabeth stated, "and I won't leave without my sister."

"We will try to send help," the fairy declared. Then, looking at the tables, she added, "Don't eat the pies. They'll make you sleepy!"

From out in the main chamber, Elizabeth could hear a great commotion. She moved to the doorway to see what was going on out there. To her surprise, she saw gnomes mixed in with the hundred or so goblins. Tables were overturned, bowls were broken, and a slick of sweetberry goo was everywhere. She wondered if she could get through that mess to warn everyone. She had an idea and, pulling her journal from her backpack, she started writing as fast as she could.

Looking around the make shift kitchen, Elizabeth tried to discover a way to escape. There was an open cupboard against one wall. She pulled on it, hoping it concealed a passageway to freedom. As it tipped forward she could see only a solid wall behind it, and something clattered off one shelf. Spectacles. She hadn't seen anyone wearing them, but picked them up and tucked them into her pack to keep them safe.

⌘

"Attack!" Randolph shouted from the walkway above the open cave. His gnome force suddenly appeared, surrounding the goblins, and pelting them with stones from every direction.

Emily was only a few feet from Randolph, and had tried to stop him before he yelled. Too late. Confusion erupted, below, as goblins and gnomes went after each other with the tools at hand: spoons, bowls, axes, table legs, and rocks. The gnomes had brought weaponry and the element of surprise, but the goblins had an ogre.

The Ogre King burst into the open cave roaring and throwing little people out of his way. His roar was like thunder echoing through the caverns. His long arms swept both gnomes and goblins aside without care. Several gnomes tried forming a ladder, standing on top of each other's shoulders, to challenge him, but a swift kick sent them all flying.

"Gunners!" Randolph yelled to his men. "Fire on the ogre!"

The gnomes had set up two of their mechanical rock shooters on the upper walkway beyond where Randolph stood. They were strategically placed where they could fire on the whole area, below. Anyone wanting to attack them would also have to make their way up the narrow path, and past Emily.

"Firing!" The gunners yelled.

The gunners delivered a hail of rocks with amazing precision, hitting the ogre, over and over, in the head, body, and arms. It was an impressive onslaught and the ogre roared in pain. Trying to advance on them, he was tripped up by ropes crisscrossing the cave floor. The Ogre King hit the floor hard as more rocks rained down on him. Not even stunned, he stood up, cursed at them. "You haven't stopped me," he bellowed, and lumbered from the main cave.

A group of goblins tried to climb up to the gnome gunners, only to run into Emily. She could easily defend the narrow path, as they couldn't surround her. With her height, strength, and staff, she kicked, pushed, and threw them off the ledge. Randolph grinned his approval. The battle was clearly going their way.

Just then, a loud shriek echoed through the cave. Goblins cowered in fear and even the gnomes stopped at the sound. From above, a woman in black lowered herself down on what looked like a thick strand of silk cord. Her skin was pale, and as white as the cord she held onto.

"The witch!" Randolph yelled. "Gunners!"

The witch heard him, and turned her attention on the gnome firing machines. Dark energy flew from her fingers, blasting both of the machines to pieces. Wood, rocks, and gnomes flew in every direction. Emily ducked for cover behind some large rocks.

More gnomes tried to rush the witch, but she pushed them back with a dark power emanating all around her, knocking them off their feet. From a shadow at the back of the cave, a small, hooded figure ran past the witch. Like lightning, the witch's hand grasped the figure's goblin cloak. The cloak slipped free, revealing Elizabeth. She kicked and tried to wiggle free, but the witch had her ensnared with more dark magic.

With great delight, the witch said, "Gnomes! Cease your attack! I claim this human girl as my prisoner!"

Emily wasn't about to abandon her sister to an evil witch. She readied her biggest stone and sailed it toward the witch's head. The stone flew straight and fast, but was deflected by the invisible barrier.

Furious, the witch launched a bolt of energy at the rocks, mere feet from Emily's location, scattering rubble around her.

"Gnomes!" The witch repeated. "Have you no leader? I demand your surrender at once, unless you wish to see this one killed."

Emily would have rushed forward, had not Randolph's hand held her back. He touched his finger to his lips, urging her to remain quiet.

"I am here, witch!" Randolph said, while stepping out from the rocks. "Do not harm the girl. I surrender."

"Tell me, what do you care for a meddlesome human child?" the witch asked, mockingly.

"This girl is under my protection." Randolph said, walking closer. "We gnomes are not seekers of violence. We do not wish harm on any creature."

"Why then, little one, have you and your gnomes attacked my workers?"

"We believe you are conducting evil magic here, dark one, and we have come to put an end to it!" Randolph answered with bold conviction.

"Evil magic?" the witch asked, innocently. "Surely you are joking? My workers have been baking pies as a gift to the king and his people."

"The pies are poison!" Elizabeth screamed. The witch put a silence spell on her, but she continued to struggle.

The witch continued, "I have been troubled with how to deliver my treats to the king. Goblins aren't known for their baking skills, and no one would want to eat pies delivered by them. So you will be the bearers of my kitchen's abundance."

"We would never," Randolph started indignantly.

"You will," the witch answered, pointing at Elizabeth while dark energy crackled at her fingertips. "And the king will never know, because you'll all look so innocent, under my spell. Deliver the desserts to the humans, or I will make this girl a treat of my own!"

Randolph sighed in defeat. He knew the pies meant trouble, but he could not let the witch hurt the daughter of Duke Daring. The gnomes would have to comply. Under her spell, they had no choice. An opportunity to make things right would come; it had to. He only hoped that the witch would not discover Elizabeth's identity before his return.

"Very well," Randolph answered, "we will do what you demand of us."

Chapter 8

Emily paced the forest floor. "You can't be planning to help her?" she said.

"Don't you see, I have no choice," Randolph explained with a sigh. "She has your sister. What else can I do?"

Emily threw her hands up in frustration. How could this have happened? The witch had Elizabeth, and would have likely had herself, as well, had Randolph not convinced her to boldly walk out of the cave in her goblin cloak along with his men, who were now loading poison pies onto carts to be delivered to the castle guards, all under the goblins' watchful eyes. But even now, hidden behind a cluster of trees, she had to keep her voice down to avoid detection.

If she went with the gnomes and tried to warn the guards, the witch might find out and harm Elizabeth. The thought of staying behind to try freeing Elizabeth also seemed dangerous and difficult. What chance would she have against the witch? Magic blocked any attempt to attack her.

Elizabeth was always good at coming up with a plan. Emily was better at the physical side of things. A group of goblins she could whack with her staff! But she couldn't handle this with just her staff. She needed a way to send a warning to the city while finding a way to free Elizabeth. She knew she couldn't be two places at once; she was going to need help, but who? The gnomes had already tried a direct assault with no luck. She needed something more cunning.

It was as if Randolph had read Emily's thoughts. "You can't come with us," he said. "The goblins will be everywhere watching us. If you wait here, I will come back and demand your sister be freed."

Emily was growing impatient. "I can't just wait here while you and the other gnomes go commit treason. I will find a way to free Elizabeth myself."

"She's being held by a dangerous witch." He hesitated a moment, as if he wanted to give her advice. "Be careful, young Daring."

Emily quickly pulled her journal from her pack and tore a page out. Writing on it, she folded it twice and handed it to Randolph. "Give this to my father, if you can," she said, then watched him go link up with the other gnomes. She made sure to stay in the foliage as a group of goblins followed not far behind the gnomes. Hairy Foot and Stink Eye were there with them. If they saw her, they'd surely alert the witch.

Emily turned back into the forest that didn't seem so enchanted, now. She knew to stay on the paths that crisscrossed through the greenery. One of them had to lead her back into the cave. Somehow, she had to free her sister from a witch protected by a magical shield, and get past goblins and the ogre.

Her thoughts drifted to the poison pies. If the gnomes were unable to warn the city guards about the Sweetberry Pies, the whole kingdom could fall to the witch's army. But what army? Emily suddenly realized she'd only seen goblins. It didn't make any sense that those little creatures would try to take over the city. There had to be something more to the witch's plan. But what?

"Hello," a small voice said from right next to her.

Emily turned but saw nothing.

Emily asked, "Who's there, and where are you?"

"I'm right here," the voice said, as a tiny person seemed to materialize in front of her. It was a small girl, floating on wings as beautiful as a butterfly's. Light seemed to emanate from within her.

"Oh my gosh," Emily said, "You're a fairy!"

"Yes. I am Azalea of the Northern Wood Faeries. I was trapped by the witch and forced to work for her until your sister freed me."

"But now the witch has her and I have to get her out of there! Please can you help me?"

"That's why I'm here," she said. "Follow me and I will help you."

⌘

The witch's cave was roomy, although not as large as the cavern beneath it. The walls and ceiling were covered in thick web. In the middle of the room were some tables and chairs, a bookshelf, and a few odd looking devices. Books and notes were strewn about one table while the other was clean and seemed to be meant for magical experiments.

Elizabeth found herself bound in web, but the silence spell had been removed, so she could speak. "If I were free, I'd shoot you with my best arrow."

"Must you be so combative?" The witch said.

Elizabeth regarded her captor. She was actually pretty for a witch. Her skin was pale white, her hair raven black. There was something about her eyes though; they seemed empty and dark.

"You are safe as my prisoner, for now. Do you really wish to anger me?"

"Blah blah blah," Elizabeth said mockingly. "It doesn't seem very safe up here, with all this sticky, nasty stuff on your walls! You really should do some cleaning."

"Keep annoying me and I will send you back down with the goblins, or perhaps that disgusting ogre would like a new playmate."

Elizabeth could just move her feet, but not her legs. She inched along the edge of the room, trying to keep the witch talking while she maneuvered to just the right position. In the corner of the cave she spotted another venting shaft, this one larger than the one in the kitchen, and it was covered with the strange webs instead of a grate. It gave her an idea, but she would have to time it perfectly.

The witch was busy with something on the book table. Perhaps she was preparing another spell, Elizabeth thought. Better to keep her distracted from whatever she was doing.

"So," Elizabeth started, "let me see if I have this right. You're sending a bunch of pies filled with sleeping potion to the kingdom so that when the guards are asleep you can take over?"

"Something like that, yes," the witch answered. "How did you know about the sleeping potion?"

"What else would you use valerian root for?" Elizabeth answered, not wanting to give away the gnomes.

"You're very clever for such a young girl," the witch said, coming closer. "Too smart for a peasant's daughter. What is your name?"

"Elizabeth," she answered, trying to sink back into the shadows. The vent was directly behind her now.

"And what is your father's name, Elizabeth?" The witch asked somewhat annoyed.

"My father? Oh, he's nobody.

"Say, how are you going to take control of the castle and the kingdom with those goblins? I mean, what happens when the guards wake up? Won't they just shoo the pesky goblins back out the gates?"

"If you must know," the witch started.

"Oh come on," Elizabeth butted in. "Just admit I found the flaw in your grand plan. You'll be queen of the kingdom for what, four, maybe five hours?"

"As I was saying." The witch was clearly agitated, now, and it was beginning to show on her face.

"Oh blah blah blah," Elizabeth interrupted. "There you go again. What could you possibly have that will help you take the kingdom?"

The witch's eyes lit up like fiery orbs, energy crackling in her hands as she aimed them at Elizabeth.

"I have ogres!" The witch screamed as she hurled a ball of energy directly at Elizabeth Daring.

⌘

Emily followed the fairy through the forest, this time being more careful of the grabber vines and other enchanted tricks. They were following a different path than before, one that seemed to twist around behind the cave entrance. The farther they went, the forest seemed to grow darker, the trees more gnarly and twisted. A chill passed through Emily and she shuddered as something slithered into the brush next to them. Emily tightened her grip on her staff.

"It's not all flowers and lights here, is it?" Emily asked.

"No," Azalea answered, "I'm afraid there are dark places in this forest, Emily Daring. Not very friendly for young girls, or faeries for that matter."

They could hear a commotion in the forest ahead of them.

"We need to move quietly, now," Azalea said. "There is a foul smell in the air."

Azalea lead Emily off the path and into the thicker brush, giving up ease of travel for concealment. The weeds were thick and seemed to forcefully wrap themselves around Emily's ankles. The fairy could fly, but even the tree branches seemed to work against her, tiring her as she went.

They proceeded through the forest, but stopped when they heard pig-like snorting up ahead. Azalea put a finger to her lips and motioned Emily to be silent. Emily dropped to her hands and knees and crawled forward slowly through the brush. She found a large thicket she could crawl into and peered out into the forest.

She could see makeshift campsites in a small clearing ahead. They were messy, with bedding of old straw or weeds and moss. At first she didn't see anyone, then a creature walked into view. It was tall and broad shouldered. Its skin had a pale green hue and its nose was more of a snout. Having seen their king earlier, Emily knew this was another ogre.

And there were more of them.

Beyond the first one, she saw a gathering area with actual tents and tables stacked with weapons. There had to be at least a hundred ogres, and she was sure there were more nearby. Some were putting weapons onto carts while others were busy strapping on armor. It was a small army, and if there were any more like it, they would pose a serious threat to the kingdom. Emily crawled back to Azalea, making sure to move quietly.

"Azalea," she whispered, "this is bad. There is an army of ogres up here!"

"You're right, it is bad," Azalea answered. "They mean to make war on the kingdom of men!"

"We have to send a warning," Emily said, "but I can't leave Elizabeth with the witch. You need to go to the city and warn them."

"The affairs of humans are not my domain, Emily Daring," Azalea said. "But you and your sister are very brave, and we owe you a debt. I will lead you to the entrance of the witch's lair, then I'll go for help."

"Thank you," Emily said, feeling some relief.

"Don't thank me yet," Azalea replied. "The witch is both evil and dangerous, and now you will be facing her alone."

"I won't be alone," Emily answered. "I'll have my sister!"

"I fear that won't be enough," answered Azalea, "but the witch does have a weakness."

STEVEN J. THOMPSON

Chapter 9

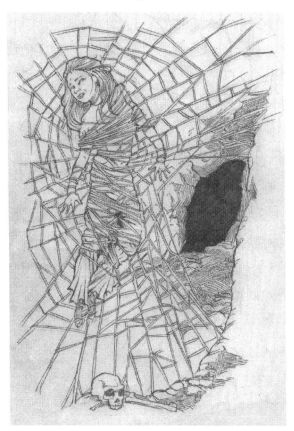

Duchess Daring was enjoying the sunlight while working in her garden. If the duke was known for his collection of weapons and his adventures, the duchess was most certainly known for her amazing garden. It stretched easily over a third of their estate, with tall hedges creating paths much like the maze outside the king's castle. There were flowers of all shapes and colors and sizes, but her garden's value came from more than just its beauty.

The duchess had learned from her mother the importance of growing herbs with medicinal and even magical effects. She had simple herbs like basil and rosemary out in plain sight, while the more mystical—even dangerous—plants were kept hidden deeper within the hedges. The untrained eye would not know what they were, anyway.

The day she met the Duke, in the Enchanted Forest, she had been gathering a particularly rare herb known for its powerful healing effects against the worst of poisons. She had carefully collected both the petals and seeds so that she could grow it in her own garden, should its need ever arise.

Her thoughts drifted back to that day with the duke. Then, as though summoned, she heard his hearty laughter as he showed off a fresh Sweetberry Pie as if it were some kind of baked trophy. Joseph clapped with joy and followed his father into the house. After weeks of going without, her husband had finally acquired his favorite treat from the guards at the city gate. She could hear him rambling on about how gnomes weren't such bad little people, after all.

The duchess smiled. The duke loved a good Sweetberry Pie and would waste no time serving himself a generous slice. She wondered if he would give a piece to Joseph first, or just start in before sharing his spoils. She could picture them both grinning from ear to ear with sweetberry all over their faces.

She put away her gardening tools and made her way inside. She had just entered the hall when she heard a loud thump in the next room, followed by Joseph crying for help. She rushed in to find the duke slumped over on the floor, snoring loudly. On the table were two pieces of Sweetberry Pie, one with a large bite taken out of it. Joseph hadn't eaten any.

"What happened?" she asked Joseph, checking her husband to make sure he wasn't choking.

"Papa was going to give me the first piece, but then he took a bite of it!"

Her mind raced as she comforted Joseph and tried to wake the duke, to no avail. She checked the pie on his plate but couldn't see anything strange. Then she saw something in the pie plate. There, just in the middle of the pie, was a rolled piece of paper that had somehow been stuffed inside. She unrolled the paper to see the word POISON. It was written in a small handwriting that she knew all too well.

How did a note in Elizabeth's handwriting get into a pie delivered by gnomes? She wondered.

Knowing, now, that the pie was the source of the duke's condition, she dipped her finger in and smelled, then took the tiniest taste. She had to know what the ingredient was in order to cure it. Even the small sample made her feel lightheaded, and she feared she'd fall asleep, as well. But as she fought off the sensation her risk paid off. She knew what ingredient had been used.

"Valerian Root!" She exclaimed. "Joseph, stay here with your father."

Valerian root wasn't actually a poison, but it did aid in bringing on sleep. Mixing it with sweetberries and a bit of magic had made a powerful concoction. Who could have cast such magic? She didn't have time to ponder this. She took her Book of Remedies from the shelf and leafed through its pages, soon finding the recipe she was seeking. The sleep spell could be broken and she had the proper herbs. But would there be enough for the duke, and anyone else who had eaten the pies?

Grabbing her garden shears, the duchess hurried out into the garden. She was searching for a particular plant, a flower that had great healing properties. It wouldn't be hidden like some of her more dangerous varieties, but in her alarmed state, she couldn't be sure where it was planted.

"There!" she exclaimed, as she came upon a beautiful row of chrysanthemums. They looked like simple flowers, but they were precisely the antidote she needed. She counted her blessings as there were at least a dozen in bloom, and collected enough to test her cure on the duke.

She rushed back into the kitchen, where she found her mortar and pestle to crush the herbs. She had the rest of the ingredients she needed and set to work grinding them all together into a powder, being careful to exactly follow the instructions in her book. Finally, she carefully measured out a dose of the powder and stirred it into a cup of water.

With potion in hand, she rushed to the duke, lifted his head, and poured a small amount into his mouth.

Duchess Daring held her husband, praying for a quick result. At first, the Duke's eyes fluttered, then he choked and coughed as he awakened. Her potion worked.

"Aryanna?" He asked. "What happened?"

"You're unharmed, my dear," she answered. "You were under a sleeping spell, but I have revived you."

"Sleeping spell?" he asked.

"Yes, it was in the pie."

"In the pie," the Duke said, still collecting his thoughts. "Those mischievous gnomes! I knew they couldn't be trusted!"

"I don't think the gnomes would do this; it's not like them," she said, "and I found this." She handed him the berry-stained paper.

"A note?"

"It was in the pie, and it's in Elizabeth's handwriting!" She exclaimed.

"How could that be? Where are the girls?" he said, his mind was racing.

"Where did you get the pie?" she asked.

"Gnomes brought the pies to the city gate, a gift for the guards and...the KING!"

Fully revived, the duke stood up and ran to the closet for his armor and sword.

"If the girls are in the Enchanted Forest, I will search for them as soon as I warn the guards!"

"Wait!" she said, "warn them about what—the pies?"

The Duke was already running out the door as he yelled over his shoulder, "The kingdom is under attack!"

⌘

Elizabeth woke, her head hurting from the witch's blast. She tried to move, but not even her toes could wiggle. Examining herself, she realized she was bound in the strange, gooey cobwebs that filled the witch's lair.

"You're awake!" the witch said.

"Yes, and I'm covered in nasty webs!" Elizabeth snarled.

"Oh relax," the witch said. "They're perfectly clean, and much softer than rope"

"So now you care about my comfort?" Elizabeth said. Her sarcasm was not lost on the witch.

"Oh, what a joy you are!" the witch said, laughing. "Such a sharp tongue in one so young!"

"Give me back my bow, and I'll show you my sharp arrows, too!"

"Ah yes, your bow," the witch said. "I noticed the crest it bears, the crest of the House of Daring. I think you've been withholding your identity from me."

"Maybe it was a gift from the Darings," Elizabeth replied, "or I simply stole it."

The witch laughed again. "I like you, child. Tell me, why did you taunt me into hurling a ball of energy at you? You realize I could have killed you?"

"I just wanted to see if you are as powerful as you said." Elizabeth shrugged.

"Perhaps," the witch said, "or perhaps you are fascinated by my magic? I saw the look in your eyes. I know the hunger I saw there."

"Hunger for what?" Elizabeth asked.

"For power!" The witch exclaimed. "Let men have their muscles and their swords. Magic is the one thing that gives a woman power over all; it empowers the weak over the strong!"

As the witch spoke energy again crackled at her fingertips. Her excitement was clearly energizing her, and Elizabeth couldn't keep herself from staring. The witch was right, she was fascinated! She imagined what it must be like to harness such energy, such power. No one, not her parents, or the King's Guards, or even her sister, could tell her what to do if she possessed such power.

Elizabeth banished the thought. The magic beckoned to her, but she resisted it. She had to concentrate on the pressing matter of discovering the witch's plan.

"I admit, you're powerful," Elizabeth said. "But why attack Highcynder? What did they do?"

"They have done plenty!" The witch yelled, as anger flashed in her eyes. "Your kingdom is not as righteous as you might think, your precious "king" not so just."

"Really?" Elizabeth prodded. "Please, do tell."

"He abandoned us, but, you're changing the subject again, aren't you? You're good at that, but now I know your weakness. You crave the knowledge and power that I wield."

"Maybe, but what does it matter? I doubt you would teach me."

"You're wrong, young one," the witch said. "Life among the goblins can be lonely, and I need an apprentice to help with my cause. Hold out your hand."

The webs around Elizabeth's arm receded, allowing her to extend her open hand. The witch harnessed the energy in her hand into a ball, dancing like a blue flame, and placed it into Elizabeth's palm. Elizabeth's eyes lit up. The sensation in her fingers wasn't painful at all, but rather amazing. As she focused, she made it dance around in her hand, bending it to her will. Elizabeth smiled at this, not noticing that the witch smiled with her.

"You have the gift for magic, Elizabeth." The witch said. "Just like your mother."

Elizabeth's concentration snapped back and the ball of energy faded away.

"But I haven't told you who my mother is." Elizabeth answered.

"Haven't you?" The witch toyed with her. "Oh, no of course not."

"You mentioned your cause. What is it you really want?"

"You really wish to know?" The witch answered. "Then I will tell you, plainly. Your kingdom is weak. King Lamont gives your people too much freedom, and a free people are given to the evils of excess. It all seems like great fun, until they find themselves wallowing in misery and chaos. I would bring them order and control. I would harness their selfish energies to be utilized for the greater good."

"But would you just tell everyone what to do?" Elizabeth asked.

"What good is freedom Elizabeth? Does it feed the hungry? Does it provide shelter? Freedom allows some to prosper while others do not. I would take a measure of their freedom, but in return give them all security and equality!" The witch exclaimed.

"And what if they refuse?" Elizabeth asked.

The witch looked at her, a wicked half-grin forming on her lips.

Elizabeth was old enough to know that other kingdoms did not give their people freedom, and that without freedom people lived in slavery. Her parents had taught her the value of freedom, and the wickedness of slavery.

Elizabeth drew a breath, ready to reply, but the witch silenced her. She waved a hand in front of Elizabeth's face, making her feel sleepy. As she drifted off, she heard the witch whisper to her, "We have company."

⌘

Emily lowered herself into the darkness. Azalea had shown her the way into the witch's lair through a small tunnel in the woods. It had the appearance of a big badger hole, and was just as creepy. Emily would never have guessed that this might lead down into the caverns below, but the faeries knew the forest well, and Azalea had assured her this was the way.

As she worked her way farther down, the tunnel opened up a bit, to where she no longer had to shinny along and could actually crawl. But as the tunnel widened it also seemed to be filled with more and more spider webs, which Emily could have happily done without! It was dark and she couldn't see any spiders, but just the thought of them skittering around made her skin crawl. She pushed her staff and her pack ahead of her to break through, and kept going. Spiders or not she was going to rescue her sister!

The tunnel was fairly straight, allowing her to see a faint light up ahead. She also thought she heard a voice. She would need to be careful now, and quiet. She inched forward until she came to a wall of webbing. The light was coming from the other side.

With her dagger, Emily carefully cut back the webbing enough to peek through. It was a large chamber with tables and a workbench holding bottles labeled in a hand she could not read. Strange globes of a mysterious light provided a soft illumination that barely reached the cave walls. She didn't see the witch, but on the opposite wall from her, covered in webs, she saw her sister.

Elizabeth! Emily covered her mouth to keep from calling out. Elizabeth was alive, or at least she appeared to be. She looked like she was asleep. She was also stuck to the wall with icky spider webs! Emily cut through the rest of the webbing blocking the shaft, and crawled into the open cave. There was rubble on the cave floor in front of the hole she came through, as if it had only recently been opened. There was still no sign of the witch, but she crawled the rest of the way to Elizabeth to avoid being detected.

The webs holding Elizabeth were strong but cut easily. Emily set her staff down and worked to free her sister's arms and legs, leaving the webs around her sister's body to hold her up. She then put her hand over Liz's mouth and whispered to wake her up.

"Mmmph," Elizabeth groaned through Emily's hand.

"Shhh," Emily whispered. "I'm cutting you free, keep watch over my shoulder."

"Miiiih!" Elizabeth groaned again, more urgently.

"Liz, be quiet!" Emily whispered again. "You're going to get us caught!"

"It's a bit late for that," a voice said from behind Emily. The witch was there, after all.

"I tried to tell you!" Elizabeth exclaimed, after Emily moved her hand.

Emily had turned with her dagger in hand to face the witch.

With a wave of her hand, the witch sent an energy bolt, knocked away the dagger, then lifted Emily and pulled her to within inches of the witch. As the witch waved her hand, Emily noticed an intricate ring on her finger. It was silver with a purple stone that seemed to swirl with black energy.

"So there was another one," the witch said. "My goblins were right. What is your name, child?"

"My name," she shouted, "is Emily Daring! Release me now or you will face the wrath of my father!"

"Emily, no!" Elizabeth shouted.

"Daring?" the witch asked, casting Elizabeth a knowing glance, "as in Duke Daring? So you are his daughters. How delightful! I thought you two were nobility, perhaps even worth a nice ransom, but the Daughters Daring are worth far more than that, to me!"

"You won't be getting any ransom!" Emily exclaimed. "When our father finds out you have us, he will come to rescue us, personally!"

"And I am counting on that, my dear," the witch said. "I've waited a long time to get my revenge on your parents. Now I have their children, and soon I will have their beloved kingdom!"

Though still suspended above the floor, Emily tried to reach back for her pack. The witch saw this and, with a wave of her hand, the pack was pulled from Emily's shoulders and placed at the witch's feet. Emily was then flung to the wall next to Elizabeth. As the energy held her, the webs snaked around her arms and legs like vines.

"I wonder what you wanted in here?" the witch said picking up the pack. She reached in with the hand that wore the silver and purple ring, searching the contents, until she seemed to find something.

Then she screamed.

Chapter 10

Duke Daring ran through the city toward the guardhouse at the gate nearest the Enchanted Forest. Although there were other gates that could be attacked, this one was the most likely. He hoped he would reach it in time.

As he neared the gate, he saw no activity. There were two guards, both asleep, sitting just inside the gate entrance, half-eaten slices of Sweetberry Pie beside them. One guard appeared to have a broken nose from an earlier scuffle.

As the duke surveyed the scene, a chubby boy walked up. "They're not supposed to be sleeping like that," he said.

"What is your name, boy?"

"Nathan Wormington, sir," the boy answered.

"Nathan," the Duke said, kneeling to his level, "I am Duke Daring. You know my daughters." The boy nodded and winced. The memory of Elizabeth's arrow still smarted.

"Nathan, I need you to run to the king's court as fast as you can. Tell them the kingdom is under attack! Tell them I sent you! This is of the highest importance. Do you understand?" The boy nodded, his eyes wide.

"Go now, quickly!" The duke watched the portly boy's attempt at running and shook his head. If there were time he would chuckle, but time was something he was sure he didn't have. He quickly moved to the guardhouse and pounded on the door. Receiving no answer, he tried the knob but it was locked.

The guardhouse not only housed an extra reserve of city guards, but also protected the windlass that was used for raising or lowering the portcullis. For a single man, lowering it would be fast and simple, but he had to reach the windlass to do it.

A horn sounded from outside the gate. The duke knew the sound well. It was an ogre war horn, followed by the heavy footsteps of an approaching army. Time was definitely something he no longer had.

Taking a step back and lowering his shoulder, the Duke rammed into the door with all his might. The door stood firm and sent the duke bouncing back onto the ground. Determined, he brushed himself off and tried again. The door did not budge.

"Perhaps we can help?" The small voice seemed to come from the ground.

The duke looked down to see a pair of gnomes, dressed in battle gear, standing at his feet.

"Gnomes!" the Duke roared. "You brought the pies that poisoned the guards, and me!"

"Yes, my apologies Sir Daring," the gnome answered, "but now we are here to help."

"Help?" The Duke said furiously. "I should sooner trust a foul goblin!"

The Duke grabbed the little fellow by his armor straps and held him up against the wall, face-to-face.

The little man reached into his pocket. "Your daughter said to give you this." He held out a slip of folded paper.

"My daughter—where is she?" He dropped the gnome to read the note. "It says you're Randolph, and that I should trust you."

The sound of the approaching army grew louder. "There are goblins out there, Sir Daring," Randolph said, motioning toward the gate, "and ogres. Please let us help!"

"How?" The duke asked.

"That window, above the door," Randolph answered. "Quickly, toss us through!"

"Find the windlass and lower the iron gate!" The Duke said as he hoisted the gnomes, who were rather light, despite their armor. "I will hold the entrance."

"Sir Daring, the witch is behind this. She has your daughter," Randolph said, then disappeared through the window.

The duke shook his head and fought back tears. How could the witch have one of his daughters, and where was the other one? Rage coursing through him; the duke unsheathed his sword. It gleamed in the sunlight as he hefted it before him. He turned toward the gate just as an ogre scout rushed the entrance shouting a battle cry.

It was an ugly creature, with long, filthy hair and bulbous warts on its chin and nose. This ogre was small for its kind, but still it stood a foot taller than the Duke. It charged him with a short axe in each hand, swinging wildly.

The duke spun, swinging his sword in an upward arc that disarmed the ogre of one of his axes, along with a chunk of his arm. The two clashed again; axe clanging into sword with an impact that shook the Duke's arm. The ogre kicked at the duke, only to feel the sting of the duke's sword upon his leg. The duke returned the kick to the stumbling ogre, sending him sprawling back through the city gate.

The ogre army was approaching the gate now, with the first rank only yards away. The duke looked with alarm at the portcullis, still overhead. He positioned himself in the middle of the entrance and brandished his sword. This was where he would make his stand.

Seeing the city gate guarded by only one man, the ogres roared and advanced. It appeared this would be their moment of victory. They would take The Shining City and put their own king upon the throne. Two steps into their march, their front ranks were pelted with rocks! A stream of igneous orbs rained down onto them from above, hitting them in the legs, bodies, and heads.

The Duke looked for the source of the rocks and saw, on top of the city walls, two gnome contraptions, one on each side of the gate. The gnomes worked them, aiming and pedaling as pulleys and wheels whipped out a shower of punishing rocks onto the ogres below.

The ogres wore heavy armor, but some of the rocks were larger than goose eggs and hurled with amazing speed. In the seconds that they stopped to shield themselves, the duke pulled the wooden doors shut and braced them with a large wooden beam. He had hoped for the iron portcullis to come down, but it remained high above the entrance.

"Sir Daring!" a voice called out from behind him.

The duke turned to see a captain of the King's Guard approaching with barely a dozen troops. He had hoped there would be more.

"Are these all the men you can spare?" the duke asked.

"The rest are defending the other gates," the captain responded, "or asleep. The pies showed up just in time for a huge lunch banquet. Nearly all of our knights fell prey."

"And the king?"

"He did not eat the pie, thank the heavens. The cooks found a warning in his."

Elizabeth, the duke thought, wherever you are, when the city is safe, I will find you.

"Captain!" the duke commanded, "get your best archers on the city walls and help those gnomes! Have the rest secure the gate, we must hold them back here or the city is lost!"

The captain had no sooner given his orders than they heard the firing of the ogres's catapults.

⌘

Elizabeth Daring watched in awe and horror as the witch crumpled to the cave floor, shrieking with pain. Dark, purple energy flowed out of her and into Emily's backpack on the ground. As the energy flowed out of her, it appeared as if the witch was growing larger.

She looked over at Emily, who was still stunned from the witch's magic and held fast by the webs. Her own binding had mostly been cut through, however, and she went to work on what was left with an arrowhead she kept tucked in one of her pockets.

"Emily," she whispered. "Emily! Wake up!"

Emily stirred. "I'm awake. What's happening?"

"She reached into your bag, and now this," Elizabeth said, "What did you do?"

As they watched the witch started to change form. Her body grew while her face crumpled in and sprouted black hairs. Her human arms and legs shrank into her body as eight new, spiny legs sprouted out of her sides. As the dark energy flowed from the witch into the bag, she was changing into a giant spider!

Elizabeth finished cutting herself free and started on Emily. It wouldn't be long before the witch finished her transformation and Elizabeth worried that dealing with the spider-witch would be much worse.

"Elizabeth," Emily said, "the faeries told me the witch's ring was the source of her power! Periwinkle must have snatched it from her!"

"But why is she changing into a giant spider!?"

"I don't know, where's Periwinkle now?"

The girls looked at the bag together, which was now actively moving and the spider-witch's eight spiny legs were coming dangerously close to trampling it! Suddenly, the bag opened and a familiar little face appeared.

"Periwinkle!" Emily shouted. "Get out of there!"

The little gnome climbed out of the pack, sad to be leaving Emily's snacks behind, but now holding the magic ring which looked huge in his small hands. The spider-witch was too close for comfort and he made a dash for the hole in the wall that Emily had entered through earlier.

The spider-witch had finished changing. She was completely spider now, with big black eyes and enormous fangs. She saw the gnome running away with her ring, and started chasing him.

"Run, Periwinkle," Emily screamed. "Run!"

Periwinkle ran for the opening but the spider-witch was faster. She slammed a spiny black leg down in front of him, cutting him off from his escape. He turned to run the other way but she blocked him there, as well. He was trapped beneath her. She looked down at him, her fangs protruding, ready to attack. She would have her ring back, and the gnome would be a tasty snack.

Whoosh! An arrow shot through the air, hitting the spider-witch in one of her many eyeballs!

"Get away from him, you witch!" Elizabeth shouted defiantly, her bow already nocked with the next arrow.

The spider-witch shrieked with pain and anger. Without the ring, her magic shield was gone, leaving her vulnerable to the young archer's arrows. She spun around, her body crashing into the cave wall, causing it to collapse over the exit hole. Emily and Elizabeth both fired upon her and she retreated into the darkness.

"She won't be gone long," Emily said. "We've got to get out of here!"

Elizabeth pointed across the room. "The other entrance, where she brought me in; it leads down into the main cave, but it's our only chance!"

"Are you all right?" Emily asked Periwinkle, grabbing up her backpack as he climbed back inside.

"Well, since you asked," he started, "I very much do not appreciate being jostled and thrown about, and I certainly do not like being almost eaten by a giant spider! Furthermore..."

The little gnome kept talking but Emily closed the backpack and threw it over her shoulder. She could hear him complaining still, although muffled now.

"Ready?" Elizabeth asked.

"Let's go!" Emily answered.

The sisters proceeded warily. Their safety was not yet guaranteed. Finding the opening in the cave floor leading down into the main chamber was not difficult. However, most of the goblins were still in it. Though their work was done, they were aimlessly waiting for new orders.

The sisters heard a crash back in the witch's lair. Something large had been knocked over, followed by glass shattering on stone. The spider-witch shrieked, and the sound of her awkward movements grew louder.

Elizabeth looked at strand of webbing leading down into the chamber. She had climbed ropes before, but this was from a much greater height. She felt her heart pounding, and her hands starting to sweat, as she looked down below.

"We're trapped!" Elizabeth said. "I can't go down that way!"

"Yes you can Liz!" Emily answered. "We're the Daughters Daring, we can do this!"

Grabbing the long thick strand of web that trailed down into the lower cave, Emily wrapped her arms and legs around it and slid down. Seeing her sister's courage, Elizabeth grabbed the web and slid down after her. Neither could resist screaming on the way down.

The sight of two human girls sliding down from the witch's lair was strange to the goblins. They had been told to guard the entrances, but not the witch's lair. Still, goblins were not trusting of humans and they picked up sticks and rocks to meet these new foes. By the time both girls had landed, they were surrounded.

The goblins paused momentarily regarding the two. Emily and Elizabeth stood poised, weapons ready, but the silence was broken by the echoing shriek of the spider-witch above them.

"Goblins!" Elizabeth shouted, "The witch has been attacked by a giant spider, and now it is coming for you!"

At that moment, the spider-witch emerged and started climbing down the web. The goblins went into a panic at the sight of the creature descending through the ceiling. They had never seen such a gigantic spider. They ran in terror, falling over each other in their effort to flee.

Emily and Elizabeth took advantage of the confusion and made their way to the upper tunnel leading out. Behind them, several of the braver goblins had taken up arms against their giant foe. One of them even managed to climb up on the spider-witch's back, and was hanging on for his life as the furious spider-witch bucked and jumped and tried to shake him off. It was such a sight that the other goblins stopped running around to watch and cheer for their heroic fellow goblin. It was a giant spider rodeo. The furious spider-witch kicked at them, at first, then began wrapping them in sticky web.

"Let's get out of here."

Chapter 11

Duchess Daring walked cautiously into the Enchanted Forest. She had taken a secret path into the forest that neither her daughters nor her husband knew about. She knew all the paths leading into the forest, and many of the paths within. Still, she walked with caution. Anyone who truly knew the forest knew the paths were the only way of safety, while even a step or two off the path placed the traveler at the whim of the forest itself.

There was also the matter of the ogres. She had avoided the gate where they were launching their attack, but she could not be sure they wouldn't have scouts surrounding The Shining City. It was unlikely though, that they knew of this particular path, and so far she had seen no sign of them.

As she ventured farther she passed beautiful forest flowers. Trillium and cardinals, Violets and hepatica, and even bloodroot. Under other circumstances she might run her fingers through them and collect some for her apothecary shelf, but the circumstances now were most dire. Her kingdom, her home, and most importantly her daughters, were in grave danger.

It had pained her to leave Joseph with a governess, but it would have been too dangerous to bring him with her. If she was successful The Shining City would soon be much safer. For now, she had to put aside her thoughts of her home and her son, for her daughters and her kingdom needed her.

The duchess soon came to an ancient tree, a towering Highcynder Oak. Its branches reached up into the sky giving shade and shelter to everything below. She stopped here to whisper secret words, calling to an old friend.

"Lady Daring?" A small voice answered.

"Iris, is it you?" The Duchess spoke normally, now. "It's me, Aryanna!"

A regal-looking fairy appeared in response. Her apparel, beautiful in purple and gold, floated around her as if under water. A warm light emanated from within her, filling the duchess with feelings of love and calmness. Iris was a friend the duchess had known since childhood; they'd been introduced when her own mother brought her into the Enchanted Forest. Years later, it was Iris who had lured the handsome Duke Daring in their direction.

While the memories of their shared past together brought joy to the duchess's heart, it was also a sad reminder of the distance that had grown between them. It had been years since she had seen her childhood friend.

"Aryanna Daring," Iris said somewhat coldly, "it is good to see you again, even in dire times."

"Then you know?" The duchess responded. "Highcynder is under attack, and my daughters are in danger!"

"As are my daughters." Iris said. "The ogres have been here for quite some time, now. They kidnapped our kind and imprisoned them!"

"Iris, why did you not send word?" The duchess said. "We would have sent aid!"

"Word was sent, my friend," Iris answered, "and summarily dismissed by the King. Lamont has grown careless in his old age. I tried reaching out to you as well, but your window of late has been closed to the songs of faeries."

The duchess's eyes dropped at the truth in the fairy's words. She had spent so much of the last decade worrying about the affairs of men, and raising her children, that she had lost her connection with the world around them. Clearly, Iris was hurt by it; faeries were extremely sensitive beings.

Another fairy burst through the leaves above, flying to them with haste.

"My Queen!" cried the messenger fairy, stopping suddenly to bow.

"Azalea was the last to see your daughters," Iris said. "It was the young one saved her from the witch."

"The witch!" The duchess and Iris shared a look of recognition. "That explains the poison pies, but not how she could have come back."

"She always craved power," Iris said. "And blamed you for so much."

"The witch sent the ogres to attack The Shining City!" Azalea interrupted, still catching her breath.

"Azalea, where are my daughters now?" the Duchess asked.

"The younger one was captured," Azalea said, "So I showed the older one a path leading down into the witch's lair, into a great cavern! I would have gone with her, but she sent me here to get help. I flew as fast as I could!"

"My girls are in terrible danger. Iris I need your help."

"We will accompany you to the witch's lair, my friend," Iris said, "and do what we can to rescue your daughters."

"I'll do that," the Duchess said. "I need your help elsewhere."

Iris frowned. The witch was dangerous, and the duchess was an old friend, no matter how angry she was with her. What could be more important than rescuing her daughters?

"What can we do to help you?"

"Save The Shining City."

⌘

Duke Daring commanded the defense at the city gate. He called out orders, adjusted the archers' fire, and personally manned defenses. The ogres repeatedly pummeled the city, especially at the forest gate. The few archers and gnomes in his company managed to slow the ogres down a little, but the duke knew that the huge doors, a solid defense against men—wouldn't hold up against the ogre horde much longer.

He had fallen back to the guardhouse to regroup, hoping desperately for more troops, while shouting orders to the guard next to him, over the sounds of battle. That was when he heard the whistling sound of the ogres's catapult fire coming directly for him! He ducked for cover but was still caught in the blast.

The duke was stunned, and his ears were ringing. He was lying in boards and debris from the guard house. A boulder from the catapults had landed next to him. The impact had smashed a section of the guardhouse, throwing men and debris in all directions. The guardsman, who he had been giving orders, lay unconscious nearby. In his haze, the duke thought the battle might be lost.

Then he felt many hands lifting him up and brushing him off. He opened his eyes to see several townsfolk around him. They had armed themselves with gardening tools or whatever weapons they owned or could get hold of.

"What are you doing?" the duke asked.

"Defending the city!" said one who was clearly a farm worker. "It's our home, too."

Behind the farmer, a blacksmith was handing out swords and poleaxes from a small cart. Several of the men had hunting bows. As they stepped forward, more citizens were showing up to fill the ranks.

Tears of pride stung the duke's eyes. "All right, men! In the name of the King, I commission all of you as Highcynder militia!

Those of you with arrows get on that wall and return fire! Pole arms behind the gate! The rest of you, fall in behind them!"

The duke's heart swelled as the citizens ran to their positions like trained soldiers. They were brave, but they had yet to face a real shockwave of attacking ogres. The first few rounds of catapult fire were mostly meant to find its range and scare the occupants within.

As the duke expected, the ogres hit the wooden doors with a battering ram. They smashed into the solid wood again and again. The hinges started to falter. It would not be long before the ogres broke them down.

With a great burst of dust and splinters, the doors came off their hinges and crashed to the ground. A wave of ogres poured through the open gateway, wielding axes and curved swords, screaming their vicious battle cries.

The ogres were a formidable sight, standing half again as tall as men and twice as wide. They were armed with large, menacing weapons and clothed in full battle armor. Their faces were covered in war paint and their long hair braided behind their shoulders. The duke could see terror in the faces of his militia. If he didn't act quickly, they would retreat, and the city would be lost.

"Defend The Shining City!" the duke yelled, as he threw a spear into the chest of the first ogre. "For Highcynder!"

"For the King!" the others yelled, regaining their resolve to defend their home. They charged forward and met the ogres head on.

Duke Daring led the charge, sword swinging. If the ogres were to take the city, he would not make it easy for them. If this was to be his last stand, he would fight with honor and courage.

With several swings of his sword, he cleared a path to the gate. The other fighters fell in behind him, pushing the ogres back! For a moment, the duke thought they might succeed in finding a makeshift barrier for the gate entrance. That moment did not last.

With an echoing roar and an enormous crash, a section of city wall exploded inward, throwing the duke, several villagers, and even a couple of ogres to the ground. Before them stood the Ogre King, with a huge hammer in one enormous hand, and he appeared ready to destroy another section of wall. He was twice the size of a man. The other ogres looked small beside him.

"This could take all day," the Duke said.

⌘

Emily and Elizabeth rushed through the upper levels of the cave. It was dark and they had lost precious time finding a torch to light their way towards the surface. The sound of battle between the spider-witch and the goblins had subsided. It was replaced with the sound of giant spider legs running and slipping over the cave floor behind them.

"Come on, Elizabeth," Emily said, looking back over her shoulder. "We've got to hurry!"

"I know," Elizabeth huffed. She was still weak from the witch's blast that had knocked her unconscious earlier, and running uphill through the cave wasn't easy. Elizabeth felt a chill at the thought of what the giant spider would do if she caught them.

"Em, thanks for saving me. I was mean to you. I'm sorry for that."

"I had to save you, Liz. We're sisters; we stick together."

"Hey, look."

Having passed a final bend in the tunnel, they could see light ahead, but it was still yards away, and they could hear the spider-witch scampering ever closer behind them.

"Liz, come on!" Emily said, running for the opening.

The sisters ran out into the light, straight into the arms of waiting goblins. They struggled but it was no use. They were trapped.

Two familiar goblins stood over them: Hairy Foot and Stink Eye. They had just returned from their pie delivery mission and had the good luck of catching the girls as they came out of the cave.

"Look, Stink Eye!" Hairy Foot exclaimed. "Human girls still here!"

"Yes, yes!" Stink Eye answered. "No escape this time. Make witch happy!"

"Her pack!" A raspy voice called from the darkness of the cave. "Bring me her pack!"

The goblins looked at the cave a moment, unsure of the voice but afraid not to comply. Stink Eye pulled Emily to her feet and grasped the pack. It was futile, but Emily still struggled, and the pack fell to the ground. Periwinkle came rolling out, along with the ring.

"My ring!" The witch called out. "Bring it to me!"

The ring rolled in front of Hairy Foot but he accidentally kicked it and sent it rolling again. Several goblins began chasing it as it bounced between their clumsy fingers. When it rolled in front of Elizabeth she saw her chance to grasp it.

"Liz, no!" Emily screamed

Elizabeth reached out for the ring, only to have it batted away by a wooden staff. The ring bounced into the darkness of the cave. Elizabeth looked up to see a familiar face as Duchess Daring stood over her. She was flanked by Azalea and a small group of gnomes.

"Mother!" Elizabeth said, "I almost had the ring!"

"The ring is cursed, Elizabeth," the Duchess answered. "You and your sister get behind me. Now!"

The duchess reached into her own satchel and retrieved a small vial. As she lifted her arm to toss it, goblins and gnomes all stepped back. She threw the vial. At the mouth of the cave, it shattered and burst into a bright, burning light, revealing the spider-witch.

"Daring!" The witch shrieked, her hand over her eyes. Seeing her now, the goblins and gnomes moved back even farther. Reunited with her ring, she had partly returned to human form, but from the waist down she was still a giant spider. The flickering flames in front of her made her giant shadow dance on the cave walls behind her. Her ring flickered too, but weaker now.

"Losing control again, Evelyn?" the Duchess said.

"Not until your annoying children came into the forest," the witch said, coldly. "I should have known these were yours, duchess."

"Why are you here, Evelyn?" the duchess asked. "Why have you attacked Highcynder?"

The spider-witch's eyes lit up in anger. She rushed forward until she was in the light. Elizabeth could see that the direct sunlight was painful for her, although she tried to hide it.

"You know why I'm here Aryanna!" Evelyn answered. "To lay claim to all that is mine. You and your king will pay for what you did to me!"

"You will lay claim to nothing," the duchess replied forcefully. "My husband will defend The Shining City. Your self-inflicted maladies are all your own."

"Liar!" Evelyn screamed. She raised her arms and fired a bolt of crackling dark energy at the duchess, who was ready for the attack.

She held a small crystal in her hand and threw it at the witch's dark energy. The crystal hovered momentarily, soaking up the witch's bolt.

Azalea dashed in and punted the crystal toward the spider-witch. It exploded on impact with the ground in front of her.

The spider-witch was stunned and stepped back into the cave. Her anger and better judgment both tugged at her. She had planned on a confrontation with the duchess, but not like this. She was weak from transformation.

The fairy tipped the scales against her. She would have to retreat.

"You can't win this battle, Evelyn," the duchess said. The transformation has weakened you, and your goblins have fled. Give up this madness and surrender."

"I will never surrender to you, duchess," the spider-witch spat the words, "and I will remember this day. You and your daughters will pay!"

Whack!

Evelyn stopped talking when a rock hurled into her chest.

"Get out of here, witch!" Emily yelled. "Leave now, or my sister will fill you with arrows!"

"It wouldn't be difficult," Elizabeth said, drawing back her bowstring. "You're certainly bigger than a chubby boy's backside!"

With a look of disgust the spider-witch slunk back into the cave and disappeared into the darkness once more. Azalea cheered and threw tiny sparklers into the air. The gnomes danced. The duchess grabbed both of her daughters and held them close to her.

"Mother!" Emily said, beginning to tear up, "I thought we'd never see you again."

"Shhh," the duchess answered. "You're safe now."

"Hmmph," Elizabeth snorted. "I don't see why she's crying. I was captured by that nasty old witch-spider thing!"

Emily gave her a look. "And I helped you escape."

"I'm relieved that you're both safe." Their mother held onto both of them a bit longer.

"When we get home," the duchess said, "you two will be explaining to your father and me just how you ended up out here."

Emily looked around a moment, then said, "Where is Father? Is he all right? Is the city safe?"

The Duchess sighed, "Your father is still defending The Shining City. He has limited troops because so many are asleep from the poison pies. I have sent the faeries to help."

"Did my message save anyone?" Elizabeth asked.

"It helped, dear. We need to return home now. Stay quiet and alert. The ogres may have the city surrounded."

⌘

Duke Daring ducked as the Ogre King's hammer swung past him, smashing through wood and stone. It wedged for a moment, giving the duke the opportunity to slash his opponent across the back. It only enraged the enormous creature, who responded with a backhand blow that sent the Duke rolling.

The Ogre King freed his hammer and continued after the duke. The king's champion stayed ahead of the violent hammer. Finally, the brute caught up to him, his hammer raised and ready for a killing blow. The duke held up his sword but knew it was no match for the powerful hammer.

Before the ogre could make the killing blow, the iron gate came crashing down onto his head.

The battle had been so heated that the Duke had forgotten about the portcullis. It was built as a buffer against invasion, not as a crushing object for large ogres, but in this case it worked. The Ogre King was knocked to the ground and run through by the iron spikes of the portcullis. He was no more.

"Hello down there!" Two gnomes called down from overhead. "Is everyone all right?"

The duke looked up to see Randolph and his companion sliding down a rope from the outer wall. They were covered in dirt and grease, the source of which he could only imagine.

"I'm fine, thank you," the Duke answered, then pointed to the Ogre King, "but he's not doing so well."

"Oh dear," Randolph said, "you're right. He doesn't look well at all!"

"He's really the least of our worries now," the Duke continued, "since you've trapped us on the outside of the city gate, along with the rest of the ogre army."

"It wasn't us," Randolph said. "The windlass gave way when another ogre boulder smashed into it."

The remaining ogre army was only a short distance and closing. There were easily enough of them to overrun the duke and his gnomish companions. Seeing only one lone defender at the gate, even if he had defeated their leader, gave them new courage. They brandished their weapons and smiled at their soon-to-be prey.

"Randolph," the Duke said, "you have proven your loyalty to Highcynder today, and I thank you for your service. But there is one more thing I must ask of you."

"Yes, Lord Daring?"

"You spoke of my daughters, earlier," the Duke continued, "I beg of you, go and help them. I will cover your escape, but please, go now!"

Before Randolph could answer the sound of the portcullis being raised interrupted him. As it rose, he could see dozens of armored men on the other side.

"I'm afraid that won't be necessary, my lord," Randolph said, smiling up at the duke.

Before the gate finished rising, the King's Royal Guardsmen began pouring out onto the battlefield. These were not the battle-weary villagers who had formed the duke's militia, but trained knights and soldiers. Their armor and weapons were polished steel that gleamed in the sunlight. Some were on horseback and others on foot. On the wall above them, the same number in archers took position, and aimed their arrows at the ogres.

"Duke Daring!" The captain of the guard called out, as he rode up on a large quarter horse. "I thought I might find you here. My men will take over this fight, now, sir."

"Thank you, captain," the duke said. "But how did you overcome the sleeping spell? Was it my wife?"

"This might sound strange, but we were awakened by faeries," the Captain answered. "I'm afraid I have not seen the duchess."

"It has been a strange day, captain."

As the Duke turned to go, the captain lined up his men and ordered surrender from the defeated ogres. The day was won, and The Shining City was safe once more. There was only the matter of his wife and daughters. He knelt down in front of Randolph where he could speak face-to-face.

"Randolph, where are my daughters. Tell me everything!"

"Hmmm," Randolph replied scratching his chin, "everything? I can tell you everything, but that is really a long story! I suppose I could start with the missing sweetberries, did you know that sweetberries make the most excellent pies? Wait of course you do, the only thing more legendary than Duke Daring's noble adventures is his love of Sweetberry Pie! But where was I? Oh yes, the missing sweetberries! We the forest gnomes had started on a noble quest of our own to track down the missing sweetberries when we ran right smack into the Daughters Daring and a whole slog of goblins. Can you believe that!"

"Tell me where they are!" the duke yelled in frustration.

Randolph was confused. Humans were definitely not the most logical beings! Didn't the duke realize that interrupting him would only make his story longer?

"And so," Randolph continued, "once the goblins were routed we made proper introductions."

"Father!" a familiar voice called out.

Over the years Duke Daring had fought many battles. He had faced ogres, giants, and slimy creatures that hide in dark caves. It was said that he was the most fearless man alive.

But now, hearing his daughter's voice, Duke Daring felt the hope of a father. For fathers always love their children, and value their safety more than anything else.

The duke turned to see the duchess, Emily, and Elizabeth standing before him. They were alive!

"Children!" the duke rushed forward and scooped them up in a great, fatherly hug. The duchess wrapped her arms around them, as well. Some of the townsfolk stopped to watch the family reunion, and even Randolph stopped talking, for a moment.

"Father," Emily said, "we fought the witch; she turned into a spider!"

"And I rescued the faeries and put warnings in the pies!" Elizabeth added excitedly. "I couldn't have done it without Emily. She saved me from the witch, too."

"We rescued each other," Emily said, with a smile, then hugged her sister, again."

"Then you are both heroes who have helped save the kingdom," the duke said. "I am very relieved to see you safe."

"Our girls were very brave today," the duchess said.

"What became of the witch?" the duke asked, concerned there might be another attack on the city.

"Gone," she said, then added, "for now."

STEVEN J. THOMPSON

Epilogue

Several days later, after cleaning efforts were underway, King Lamont held a royal court. Iris and Azalea of the faeries were invited, but declined to attend. Faeries still did not feel comfortable in crowded public settings. Randolph and even Periwinkle were present, along with an entourage of Forest Gnomes. The King would have liked to have had the witch there for a public trial, but a company of soldiers sent into the caves had found no trace of her.

The hall was filled with nobles and relatives of the king. His Royal Guard was well represented, along with their captain, and the entire Knight's Council. But of all the guests, there were none so welcome, and important that day, as the Darings. The duke, duchess, and, of course, their beautiful daughters. Tales of their heroic deeds had spread throughout the kingdom, and the king wanted to publicly award them for their uncommon bravery.

The duchess and her daughters wore the finest of dresses, sparkling radiantly in the light of the court. Even the duke and little

Joseph—beaming with pride at his sisters— wore formal attire, for it wasn't everyday one was honored by the king for bravery. The Darings had much to be proud of.

It was truly a day of celebration, with plenty of food and music. Musicians played on flutes and harps in the background, while servers brought out platters of fine meats and cheeses. Annie Whipperpeel was there as well, arranging an assortment of baked goods for more servers to feed the celebrating crowd. Elizabeth watched her intently, sure that something with Annie was amiss but unable to put her finger on it. She was just starting to feel hungry when the trumpets sounded the king's arrival to call the court into session.

A captain stepped forth and called the duchess forward.

"Your Majesty," she said, as she curtsied before the royal throne.

"Cousin!" the king greeted her, heartily. "I am told you are responsible for the faeries giving aid in our time of peril."

"I merely asked them," she said, modestly.

"Nonsense!" the king retorted. "Your diplomacy saved us all. Had the faeries not revived our soldiers when they did, I shudder to think what would have happened to The Shining City and all of Highcynder."

"Thank you, Your Majesty," she answered. "You honor me."

"But your actions, and the faeries' absence today, points out that we must strengthen our relations with them. I wish for you to become my ambassador to the Fairy Folk, in hopes that our people and theirs can establish a new friendship. Will you accept this task?"

"As you wish," the Duchess answered. "I would be delighted."

The audience cheered and clapped. The promise of a new friendship between humans and faeries was something to celebrate, indeed!

Then the captain called forth the gnomes. Randolph stepped forward, unsure of courtly ways. Periwinkle was nowhere to be seen.

"Um, hello, Your Majesty." Randolph said, while fingering his tall gnome hat, nervously.

"Randolph of the Forest Gnomes," the king said, in all seriousness, "are you the leader of your people?"

"Well", Randolph started, "we don't actually have titles of authority, but I am the "unofficial" leader as it were. It all started one day when the Gnomish High Council got together and realized that we had no official leadership. Even the high council was just a gathering of any gnomes who chose to show up to meetings – usually the ones who weren't already engaged elsewhere."

"AHEM." The king interrupted.

"Yes?" Randolph asked, looking a little annoyed at the king.

"I have called you here," the king continued, "to answer for the activities of the gnomes in recent days and decide on your fate. Was it or was it not you who delivered the poisoned pies, placing our kingdom in terrible danger?"

The room went silent as the audience was clearly stunned. Emily shook her head, ready to shout her defiance, but her father cautioned her with a stern look, then stepped forward, himself.

"Your Majesty," he began, "the gnomes aided us in our moment of peril. This one personally helped me defeat the Ogre King!"

"Duke Daring," said the king, "your bravery is well noted, and I appreciate your words on behalf of the gnomes. This is why I have decided on banishing instead of imprisoning them."

"But Your Majesty!" the duke exclaimed.

"I'm sorry," the king said, raising a finger to silence the Duke. "Is there anyone else here who would speak on behalf of these gnomes before I declare judgment?"

"We will." Elizabeth said as she and Emily stepped forward. "The Daughters Daring will speak on behalf of the gnomes, Your Majesty."

The king hid a smile and winked at the Duke. This had been his plan.

"Very well, Daughters Daring," the king said. "I will listen to your arguments, but know this. If you do not convince me of their innocence, you will forfeit whatever rewards I have planned for you today. Do you still wish to stand for them?"

Everyone watched silently, waiting for the girls to reconsider. Why would anyone give up fame and fortune for some pesky gnomes? The girls stood their ground next to

Randolph, and did not budge. The duchess stepped forward, as well, to be by their side with the duke.

"All right," the King sighed. "What can you say in their defense? These gnomes poisoned my guards, putting the city in peril. One act of heroism cannot erase an act of treason."

"But a series of heroic deeds can save the day," Elizabeth said. "The gnomes were forced to deliver the pies by the witch. She held a terrible ransom over their heads, which they could not ignore."

"And what, young Daring, would that ransom be? A mountain of socks?" The audience chuckled at the king's joke.

"She had my sister!" Emily Daring said sternly. The audience went quiet again.

"Your Majesty," Elizabeth continued, "In our rescue of the faeries, I was captured by the witch. She threatened me and demanded that the gnomes deliver her pies. Randolph could not allow any harm to come to me, so he did as she demanded."

The king paused and looked at Randolph.

"Is this true?" he asked.

"Yes, Your Majesty," Randolph answered, the hat now still in his hands.

The king sat quietly for a moment, contemplating their report of events. If it were true, there would be no justice in banishment, and he believed himself a wise and just sovereign.

"Randolph, leader of the gnomes," the king said, solemnly, "in light of your heroic deeds, as reported in this hall, and for so valuing the life of one of our own precious heroes, I declare you forgiven, and welcome you to share in a treaty of friendship with our kingdom!"

The audience cheered, relieved that the little gnomes would be spared. Still, there were some in the audience who were sure that the gnomes were responsible for their missing socks.

Finally, the Darings were called forward. The duke, duchess, Emily, and Elizabeth all stood before the king. Joseph held his mother's hand, and played with the ornaments on her gown.

The king stood, which gave even greater import to his words. "I am pleased to honor Highcynder's bravest hero, and especially the Daughters Daring, our newest heroes, who faced great danger yet stood in loyalty to their kingdom. Without them, the battle against the invading ogres surely would have been lost.

You have shown not only great courage in the face of danger, but courage to stand up for what you believe to be right, even at the risk of annoying your king. You are all to be awarded with medals of bravery, your deeds shall be recorded in the royal library, and a tournament of knights shall be held in your family's honor!"

The assembly cheered again. They threw confetti in the air and shouted for Highcynder and The Shining City and, of course, for the Darings. The Daughters bowed and curtsied, and helped themselves to some of the fine treats that were served, while their father held the noblemen enthralled with only slightly embellished stories of his battle with the Ogre King.

The kingdom was saved, and the mystery of the sweetberries was solved. But most importantly, Emily and Elizabeth learned a valuable lesson. They had learned not only to value each other, but also that the love of one family can make the difference against the greatest of odds, and standing together with family was what being a Daring was all about.

The End

Character Profiles

Emily Daring: The oldest daughter. Brave and athletic, but also compassionate towards others, especially animals. Emily would rather be outside participating in swords or horseback riding, if only her mother didn't insist on her wearing those bothersome dresses!

Elizabeth Daring: Emily's younger sister. Elizabeth is witty and sharp with a craving for knowledge. Sometimes stubborn, Elizabeth likes to be in charge and do things her way. Whether she admits it or not, she draws courage from her sister and her family, and when the going gets tough she stands up for what is right.

Joseph Daring: The youngest of the Daring family. Joseph is also an adventurous young lad who may someday have great tales of his own.

Duke Daring: Father and hero of the Daring family. The Duke was not born of royal blood, but instead was awarded his title for great deeds of heroism. Now a bit older, he hopes to use his notoriety and influence to help shape a new kingdom while also trying to keep his adventurous children out of harm's way.

Duchess Daring: Mother to the Daring children and favored cousin of King Lamont. What Aryanna Daring lacks in physical brawn she makes up for with a potent knowledge of the magical arts. Like her husband, she believes strongly in a new direction for their country while hoping these efforts don't distract her from the protection of her children.

King Lamont: A wise and just king, but also tired and lonely. Lamont wishes to move his kingdom towards a more representative form of government but has underestimated the dangers that lie ahead. He still grieves for the loss of his queen.

Annie Whipperpeel: Annie is everyone's favorite baker of delightful goods. It is said that Duke Daring would storm a castle full of ogres for Annie's Sweetberry Pie! But is Annie hiding a secret?

Randolph of the Forest Gnomes: The unofficial leader of the gnomes, Randolph is older and known for his wisdom among the gnomes. He and the other gnomes of the high council have seen the danger facing their human neighbors in Highcynder and seek to help, even at risk to themselves.

Periwinkle: A garden gnome who is much smaller than his forest cousins. No one knows for sure how Periwinkle came to be in their company, but Randolph seems to have taken him in. That is, until Periwinkle decided that Emily's backpack made a great home from which to tag along on her wonderful adventures.

Iris of the Faeries: A childhood friend of Aryanna Daring. Iris knows the dangers facing the faeries and wants only to keep them safe and away from the kingdoms of men. Iris feels hurt that Aryanna has been away for so long.

Azalea of the Faeries: A brave follower of Iris, Azalea meets the Daughters Daring when they rescue her from the evil witch. She wants only to return the favor.

Hairy Foot and Stink Eye: A pair of goblins now working for the witch. Goblins are small, like gnomes, but crafty in the ways of hunting and warfare. Many an adventurer has fallen prey to the goblin's traps. The Darings likely haven't seen the last of these two.

The Ogre King: A fierce and enormous creature. Ogres stand taller than men and he is bigger than his brethren. The Ogre King's only desire is to lead his army against the kingdom of Highcynder and crush the humans once and for all.

Evelyn the spider-witch: Evelyn despises King Lamont and believes him to be a weak ruler, and her past with Aryanna Daring remains a mystery. A master of dark magic, Evelyn seeks the downfall of Highcynder and the heroic Darings. She sees in Elizabeth Daring a kindred thirst for knowledge and power, but she will let nothing stand in her way. With an army of ogres and goblins at her disposal, she may yet prevail.

STEVEN J. THOMPSON

About the Author

Steven J. Thompson was born and raised in Northern California. He left home to serve in the United States Army and returned later to raise a family and complete his education. A father of three, he entertained his own daughters with bedtime stories of adventurous young girls who were not afraid to face the world. After years of service as an Army Reserve Drill Sergeant and now as a foster care worker, he is now putting these stories in print with the Daughters Daring, a new series with more to come. These are stories that encourage children, especially young girls, to be brave and daring. He and his family hope you will enjoy them.

And more to come....

Stay tuned for the next chapter in the Daughters Daring series as Emily and Elizabeth stow away on a pirate ship and once again face the minions of the spider queen in:

The Daughters Daring & the Crystal Sea

STEVEN J. THOMPSON

THE DAUGHTERS DARING

49018919R00107

Made in the USA
Charleston, SC
17 November 2015